THE GOPHERS
OF HIGH CHARITY

THE GOPHERS
OF HIGH CHARITY

KIMBERLY UNGER

First Edition
ISBN: 978-0-9970793-7-1

Ramen Sandwich Press
www.ramensandwichpress.com

ONE

She spat.

Everyone spat. The gutters of High Charity ran thick with spit and offal and the unmentionable sick of everyday life. Annie picked up the habit from Ma whose tobacco only added to the seeping stink that trickled down the streets and corners.

She hefted the brick, feeling the weight with her fingers. The roughness matched well with the calluses on her hands, the fabric of her skirts. It wasn't a whole brick; the lumpy loaf shapes didn't fly well, didn't make as much of a mess when they hit if they was whole. Bricks were immune to magic, everyone knew it, that's why all the protection charms had to be carved into the doors instead of scribed on the walls. Mutt had taken a hammer to the wall out back, giving the group a sharp-edged pile of ammunition, each piece the size of a goose egg.

Annie was looking bored. *Nuthin' gotya nicked faster than looking busy. Nuthin' worse than looking like you were "upta sumpin".* She ran a finger around the sharp edges of the brickbat, feeling the comfortable weight of two more in her pockets. Her heart was racing. A swig of Mutt's rotgut should have steadied her nerves, but all it did was make her palms sweaty. She couldn't afford to miss.

She waited for the signal, shifting her weight from foot to foot in boots too big for her feet. Dirty Mike gave the signal, always did. Annie'd been on the fringes of the Gophers before with a half dozen other kids, keeping the interest of one lad or another until she'd found someone who'd taken her seriously. One who'd given her this chance to be a part, to do the deed and get her cut after all was said and done. It was going to be her cut, *her ownself.* No lowered eyelids and hasty gropings, hoping for a handout or, better yet, a chance at a sodden drunk with a fat wallet. She was taking a step up.

Annie spat. Rude, Ma called it. *Never marry better with a filthy habit like that.* Anne didn't want to marry better. She wanted to *be* better. Not the strange smelling tight-shoed kind of old-world better Ma nattered on about. The better that involved potions and lotions and bad-smelling smoke to tell fortunes and find true love. Better here. Better now. Better than any of these meat-fisted lads who took their cut and blew it on boner-charms and nights with gals like the ones Ma warned her not to be. Better on her terms.

When Dirty Mike gave the signal, Annie said a quick prayer to the Moonlight, stepped out into the street and let the brick fly.

The throw was perfect. Hand-packed earth and lime met glass begrimed by the morning's damp and the ever-present haze of smoke from the forges. The cheap protection spells went down, Annie could feel them sizzle in the air. The flat, harsh crack drew bodies like flies to offal. Everyone with ears knew *sumpin'* was up. The driver swore, colorful and nonsensical, and the lurching shuddering wagon ground to a halt, beasties resisting the pull of the reins. Annie cheered. The workman scrambled out of the cab, blood in his eyes from where Annie's determination had struck. He went down to one knee, scrabbling in the dirt, but not overcome, he grabbed a fistful of the summer-dry dust and ground it into the wound in his forehead, staunching the flow of blood. He didn't leave the cab, instead he reached back inside and drew out a carved cudgel as long as Annie's arm and half again as thick. He wasn't staying to defend the goods, he was just there to defend the cart and horses.

Annie's little clot of friends descended. Mike's pry-bar made short work of the latches at the back of the box-shaped wagon, the doors sprang wide. From the front of the wagon, Annie stared down her victim. The shattered front window failed to diminish its presence in her eyes. A baker's delivery wagon yoked to two slab-sided, heavy-horned beasties whose eyes rolled until she could see the whites. She, a slip of a girl in skirts too short and shoes too big had brought it to a stop. No spellstuff, no big, fat muscles, just a well-placed brick and a will to take action.

The press of unwashed bodies was moving into a mob. That wasn't her business, that was for the burly ones, meaty-handed and built like hobnail boots, the ones you didn't mess with because of the sheer mass of them. Annie faded into the crowd and dodged around skinny hips and stained workpants. She couldn't resist passing within arms-length of the beasties, the driver and his charmed length of wood keeping the grimy hands of the kids off the bridles and yoke. A duck and a scramble brought her to the back of the lorry with Dirty Mike as the man inside, shoveling coarse rolls and loaves of bread out into the waiting hands that grasped at the wooden slats.

"MIKE!" Annie drummed her fists on the wooden butt of the

wagon. Mobs were never silent, she had to scream and pound. Her reward was a full fat loaf of the Baker's custom, long gone cold but the smell of it was like the gift of a clean sea breeze, it cut through the thick of the air offering a moment's relief.

A torn heel of bread followed the true prize, jagged like the brickbat that had been the source of her power, however brief. HER reward, *HER ownself*. Mike didn't use words much, but the extra handful of crust was better. Words didn't fill a belly.

The ugly started moving, she could feel it in the way the crowd shifted. What had started as a children's mob had collected too many grownups. Mike felt it too, the open line of his brows hardened, eyes gone crafty and cold. Standing in the open back of the lorry, he was above the crowd. If the King's Guard showed their faces he'd be nicked straightaway.

The chaos of the crowd was a lie told to make the Starchies bowels run cold, to chase the few better-offs back into their houses and storefronts. Mike's hard gesture, a thumb across the throat, was proof of that. Every eye in the crowd had been on Mike, and every warm body in the mass had played their part. The ugly roiled as the street cleared on Mike's signal. Annie jammed the heel of bread into her mouth, cheeks pouched like a rat with an apple. Both arms wrapped around the whole loaf, her prize, as she ran for home.

TWO

"STOP YER YELLIN!" If the trough-sized room had windows they would've suffered the same fate as the wagon's. A fist-sized brick had nothing on the power in Ma's voice, she'd been an Acolyte in another time, with a voice that carried to all the corners of the worship-hall. The boys shut their lips tight, but only long enough for Annie to take a breath. The room in the middle of the rookery was always dim and today it stank of onions. Annie felt like a savior bringing salvation home, a loaf of bread clutched tight to her chest. Her gift to the family.

Ma snatched it when she saw it, turning it over with a scowl, thumping the bottom of the loaf with a knuckle as if looking for weevils.

"Where'd ya get this?"

Annie ducked her head, shuffled her feet. The fire in her soul guttered low under the woman's gaze.

"Paid it. Helped Dirty Mike with sumpin'," she mumbled. It wasn't entirely a lie, it was her fair share. She'd done the job as asked, Mike had done the stealing. Her conscience was clear enough.

It was the wrong answer, a rough grab and a strong pull and Annie was nose to nose with the woman that had born her. The stink of tobacco wrestled with the onion, fought a duel in the space the breadth of a rat's tail between the girl and the mother. Blue eyes searched for the truth, the long, thin nose trembled as if anticipating something foul. Annie held her breath. If Ma smelt the rotgut on her breath it would be whippings and prayers to the Moonlight until eight bells.

When Ma released her it was with a calculated flip of the wrist, a not so gentle reminder that a cuff to the side of the head had been withheld for now. Annie was ready for it and answered with her own practiced twist of the feet. A step too far to the left would fetch her up against the hot stove, a step too far to the right meant a nasty encounter with the rough brick of the wall. It would have been a perfect escape except for Tate, who'd crept up behind his sister to pull at her skirts.

Annie's graceful escape turned into a pile of arms, legs, unwashed skirts and dust billowing up from between the slats of the floor. She rolled quickly, getting one hand on the toddler to yank him to his feet, the other hand freed the skirt from her knees so she would be standing to face Ma's wrath if it came down. Tate didn't have time to make a sound.

"Good catch, little man." Annie kept her voice light, bright, as if the boy had done her a service instead of a trouble. Turning her back on Ma was a risk, but if Tate started wailing, there'd be swats with a wooden spoon all around. She squared his shoulders and tugged the rough seams of his shirt straight. "Big, strong boy like you savin' a lady from a tumble,"

At three years old, Tate was an angel. Eyes that never changed out of their baby blue and light brown hair that still curled around his ears. He sniffled, tears threatening, but he wasn't too young to understand that an angry Ma would punish everyone in the room, at fault or not. Annie stared urgently into his eyes, willing him to stay quiet. He gulped and rubbed his nose with a grimy fist.

"SO big!" He grinned, the moment passing. A clatter behind her told Annie that Ma had gone back to sorting out supper. The dead-fish gaze had moved off. Annie let out a breath in a quiet sigh, to her mind, the entire room had suddenly exhaled around them. The sounds of other families in the tenement, of hawkers and carts in the street reasserted themselves. The bustle of too many people in too small a space resumed uninterrupted. They were all in for the night and Ma stitched the door closed with a blessing and a handful of genuflections. The spell wouldn't let any but the eldest brother back out onto the street after the sun went down. Annie always thought it strange behavior for a former Acolyte of Moonlight, but of all Ma's hard and fast rules, this was the biggest. *Nobody goes out when the moon is high.* This time of the year, daylight ran late, which meant that time in the rooms was short and Annie didn't mind quite so much. Winter was another matter. Short days, long nights and plenty of sour tempers. Day was where Annie belonged, brash and full of light. She wasn't as sure of herself at night.

"Git off the floor and help me get the table set." The ire was gone from Ma's voice. It was the way of things in the household. One moment you were ducking a thrashing for breathing too loudly, the next was all cakes and sunshine. Annie scrambled to her feet and went for the basket where a collection of wooden bowls and spoons was tucked safely out of the way. Da had made them, as a toddler she had worn them as hats or used them to sort out the fingertip-sized white beans that had to soak for a whole day or you'd break a tooth. The two largest were carved from the same tree, Ma had said. He'd made them when they'd first got married.

Annie sorted the bowls out onto the long planks that served as a table, the patterned linen covering the rough surface also kept splinters at bay. Spoons came next, metal for Ma and Da, wood for Annie and the rest. She set a place for every member of the family, even the absent ones. Ma insisted, and Annie knew better than to buck against this particular tradition. Somedays Ma would bring in a stranger to fill the absent space left when Da traveled to work. More often than not it was one of the old ladies who watched the littlest kids while the washing got done. It was always a lady though. Ma's charity didn't extend to the menfolk. Annie asked her about it one night when she was feeling especially bold and Ma had seemed more maudlin than angry. She didn't get an answer, just a stern finger and a shake of the head.

Annie finished with the dishes and faded away from the table. Each of the children had a job, a specific task assigned before dinner would appear. Annie was done, getting in the way of the brothers would simply cause more trouble. Instead she took up a spot on the long bench and watched.

Oldest brother Nick appeared at the door with a bucket of freshly shucked oysters. Ma sliced them with the big knife, rolled them, one by one, in soured milk and the crumbs from last week's bread and dropped them into the pan that sizzled on the top of the stove. Ten paces across the room, Annie could feel the roll of heat, the smell of frying shellfish and oil mixing and hanging in the air. It was even visible, smoke roiling upwards towards the ceiling, adding to the overall dim of the room. She flipped over and pushed the window open as wide she could so the smoke would have a way out. They were lucky to have one of the outside partitions, the "room" had a single window that opened onto the alleyway between the tenement building and its closest neighbor. Tate scrambled up onto the couch next to her, leaning out the open window as far as he could. Annie set the window's brace and kept one hand on the back of his shirt while he reached to try to touch the wall of the building across the alley. It was close enough that the older brothers, Nick and Robert, could reach across and draw marks in the soot, but Tate's fingers just grabbed at the open air.

THREE

A second pair of woolen socks fixed the problem with Annie's shoes being handed down from the ratcatcher's daughter. You didn't turn down good leather boots, even if they made your feet sweat. Being lightfooted only took you so far before a nail or an iron-clad hoof cost you a toe or worse. Annie trotted down the sidewalk, the sound of the leather soles lost in the din of early morning. Summer was coming and the washed-out sunlight was already heating the brickwork, adding the earthy smell to the street's potent mix. Breakfast was always porridge, except when there wasn't any. It might not sit well, but the gooey lump in the pit of her stomach kept it from complaining.

"Oi, Annie!" Mary fell into step beside her, the two girls alike as peas in a pod. Mary's frock was a bit more worn, hair a shade more red than brown.

"Any news, Mary?" Half-a-year older than Annie, but a fingertip shorter, Mary was part of the group that hung out back at Hopper's, waiting for the grownups to take them seriously. It had been Dirty Mike's idea to organize them, give them jobs to do, keep them from getting underfoot. It helped keep the adventurers and explorers who came through from picking up kids that weren't theirs for free labor.

"Boy do I got news!" Mary's grin lit up her entire face. "After you went home ta yer Ma, Shy Thomas came out ta Hopper's, called out Dirty Mike on account of the wagon being under the Spitters' wing."

The Spitters were a gang from three blocks over. Not so many kids over there, all grumpy old maids and angry men who dressed like Starchies but gave up their coin almost faster than they laid hands on it. The Spitters and the Gophers got along well enough most days, seeing as they were practically neighbors with only a dog's run between them. The borders always seemed to be in dispute, but Annie could never tell if that were official or if someone was *upta' sumpin'*, The Spitters were all goodfellas, con men and thieves, quick to tell a story and cheat a feller, but not so quick to run up a fight.

"Mike wouldn'ta gone after the wagon if the Baker was paid up."

Mary shrugged. Annie knew full well she was a troublemaker and a gossip, but she wasn't a liar.

"I know that, and you know that, but Thomas said otherwise, right loud and right in front of the whole bar."

The two girls moved to put their backs up against the wall as they stopped and talked. It was habit. People on the move tended to throw elbows, so an ambling pace down the side of the road had its risks.

"So what happened? All of it."

"Fists, bleedin' faces, the usual run of trouble." The twinkle in her eye and the smirk told Annie there was more to it than that.

"Oh, come ON!" She shook Mary's shoulder. "Spill it, then."

"Oh, you wouldn'a be interested, Starchie girl like you."

Annie colored, the tips of her ears flushing red. Everyone teased her because of Ma. It wasn't fair. Ma helped her keep her clothes clean and darned any holes. Nipped and tucked to make sure the hand-me downs fit right and had bits that could be let out if needed. When she'd been kicked out of the Order of Moonlight, Ma had paid the rent as a seamstress. She still put in a good half day sewing before she started in on the bottle, if the day before hadn't run on too long. She did right enough by Annie and her brothers most of the time.

Annie swallowed her anger. Mary didn't mean anything by it. Having a friend copycat the bad-apples, even in a joke, hurt a bit, hurt a lot some-days. But *having* a friend as worldly as Mary was worth keeping her mouth shut. Annie took a quick breath and focused on the question at hand.

"Oh, go on then."

"Fine." Mary never could resist a good story. "So Shy Thomas shows up at the saloon, 'cos you know, he's Thomas, he likes the saloons, and he's never sober after the sun goes down." The best part of Mary's stories was the play acting. She didn't just whisper behind her hand like some of the girls, she threw her whole self into it, like the defenders down at the Black Hall. She drew herself up against the wall until she was almost a hands breadth taller than Annie and puffed out her chest.

"I was in the alley, helping Ida figure out which guys were the best marks, 'cos you know Mike don't allow any funny business in the Hopper, so she's gotta pick them outside. Thomas comes swaggering in, and starts off all friends with Mike, upta the bar, buys a round, like they's just having a friendly drink. Then things get all shouty. I dunno what started it, but Mike gets that look. You know the one he gets before someone loses an eye? Thomas though, he's twice the size o' Mike, right?"

"Right."

"So, Thomas grabs Mike and starts shakin' 'im, which, you know, that ain't right, not in a proper fight. And then Mike says," Mary dropped her voice in a squeaky parody of a man's baritone, "YE DON'T BE CROSSIN' ME LIKE THAT." A cough and a quick thump on her chest returned Mary's voice to normal.

"So, Mike and Thomas were working together on sumpin'?"

Mary shook her head, she wasn't about to stop now that she was on a roll. "Then Thomas says, "'AIN'T ACCUSIN!', but before he's done Mike gets up and slugs him, whammo, right in the gut!"

"Not the face?"

"Nah, Thomas has that great, honkin' chin, like someone glued an old boot to his jaw. Bust yer hand on a chin like that, so Mike gut-punched him instead." The swing of her arm in pantomime nearly clipped a passerby. "And Thomas…" Here she dropped her voice to a whisper. "Thomas didn'a go down."

"Didn't go down? But Mike's the guy who punched out that ox that escaped from the shipping yard."

"Nah, he had a hammer that time, remember? An' Thomas, lookin' back at what I saw, I'm not so sure he was drinkin' at all. I think he was tryina set something up. He just stood there and laughed. Dirty Mike, ya know, he turned six colors o' red."

"And?" Annie was getting impatient. Mary usually didn't leave out the bloody bits, she was hoping for a busted nose at least.

"And *nothing*, Thomas walked out o' the Hopper. That's the WEIRD thing. Mike didn'a do nothin', none o' the boys did nothin', he *just walked out*. Mike said a bunch a nasty things to the back of his head, but no one lifted a finger." Both girls stared at each other, wide eyed for a moment.

"So, what's wrong with Mike, then?" Annie said finally. There was a cold little knot in the pit of her stomach. It turned the warm lump of porridge into a cold ball of mud. The whole story had lost its charm. Annie had been expecting a proper knock-down-drag out fight, instead she got a mystery. If Mike had lost his edge, it was only a matter of time before someone else started in bossing everyone around and Mike ended up in the river.

"That's the question, innit?" Mary was far more excited than a story without a few cracked skulls warranted. "What's Thomas got? Some kinda spellstuff that kept Mike from throwin' another punch? Or better yet, what did he tell Dirty Mike that kept him from jes kickin' his arse sideways?"

Annie considered this solemnly. Mike was a tough one, he took Annie and Mary and the rest of the kids seriously, which was something that Annie didn't want to lose. And if there was some kind of trouble for Mike, it might just be trouble for them too.

"So, what do we do?

Mary chewed on a ragged thumbnail as the girls took a turn down the alley beside the Butcher's. The stink here hung heavy in the air, thick enough for you to part with a hand if you weren't already using it to hold your nose.

"Do? We don't DO nothin' except keep our heads down. Geez, Annie, some days it's like yer my younger sister instead of my spinster friend."

Annie punched her in the shoulder none too gently. First the Starchie comment, now the spinster, Mary was in a mood to be mean.

"Not yet I'm not. That's for old, wrinkly girls."

"Like Ida?" Mary smirked. Annie laughed a guilty laugh. Ida wasn't there to hear, so there was no real harm, and Annie was relieved Mary's teasing had found a new target.

"She's not that old either, she's just puttin' on airs." Annie defended the older girl, but it was halfhearted. Speak up too loudly and the teasing would come back around to her again.

"She's anglin' you mean. Heard tell she hooked up with Ginger Leighton."

Ma would have been aghast. Ida was only two years Annie's senior, the eldest of the kids that hung out behind the Hopper. She'd taken on the role of being the boss of the gang, organizing them for Mike, sending them out in groups of twos or threes, running errands and picking pockets. Ida was getting tired of being *one of the kiddos* and was spending more time in the saloon trying to work her way up from pickpocketing to…. Well, Annie wasn't sure what she was angling for. Prostitutes and pickpockets were the rule for girl-folk, unless you convinced the Acolytes you were worth it. Ida wanted something better, just like Annie did. The fact that Ida didn't know what it was yet meant she made life hard for Mary. Annie counted it a blessing that Ida seemed to like her.

Mary led the way around the back of the building to where the courtyard lay. Like so many places in High Charity, all the shop fronts had backs to them as well. Places too small to cram a proper building into, though in some places they shoehorned them in anyways. Pretty Boy Denis owned the Hopper, and he defended the not-quite-square patch of mud and brickbats behind it from anyone foolish enough to try and camp out. It gave him a space for fights and private discussions. It was well known that Denis would have a couple of Mike's boys chuck a drunkard out into the street in front of the bar, but if you were chucked out the back you might not ever be seen again.

Ida's little group gathered here in the morning, whoever could escape the fetching or cleaning or any other sort of menial tasks that might beset a kiddo big enough to turn a doorknob. Being just a few streets away from the docks, kids unattended or too slow could get shanghaied or pressed into a job crawling into ship spaces too small for the adults. The back of the Hopper was *outta sight, outta mind.*

"Oi, Annie!" Ida was there ahead of them, kicking her heels against the disintegrating brick of the wall. She smiled, showing off teeth that were better suited to a horse in a face that was otherwise friendly enough. She hadn't really started to wrinkle yet. It was the hair that did it, Annie decided. More yellow than brown it cast a soft halo when the light hit it right, like the pictures of Lady Moonlight in the stained glass windows at the Temple.

Annie couldn't think of a single boy who wouldn't jump at the chance to do a favor for Moonlight.

"Morning, Ida! What's the news?"

The look that passed between Mary and Ida was toxic, if there had been a cow in the courtyard, her milk would have soured on the spot. Ida and Mary worked well enough together, but they didn't like each other for reasons Annie had never been able to sort out. As far as she knew, Mary had never crossed Ida. Lots of the littler crooks would listen to Mary, she had a softer touch than the haughty blonde. Ida was better at planning and organizing, everyone knew that, but she was bossy and quick with the back of her hand. Mary was always careful not to cross her openly, but that wicked tongue was always ready with a taunt or a tease when Ida wasn't within earshot.

"I got a job for you two, since yer the first ones standing. This one's right from Dirty Mike, so no mucking about."

It felt like fingertips of excitement ran up the back of Annie's spine. She opened her mouth only to be interrupted by Mary's sharp question.

"What's in it fer us?"

Annie snapped her mouth shut, feeling like a fool for not asking the question herself. First rule, set the terms, she reminded herself sternly and nodded in agreement.

Ida smirked.

"For you? What, Dirty Mike owing you a favor ain't good enough for ya?"

Annie mulled it over in her mind. A favor from Mike was no small thing, but favors could be forgotten.

"If we hear it from Mike, then it's good enough." Mary broke in again before Annie's tongue could get off its mark.

"Callin' me a liar, Mary?"

"Callin' ye quick ta hand out a favor that ain't yours, Ida." Mary returned, not to be bossed around this morning.

Ida rolled her eyes and her head bobbled in a mocking gesture. "Take my word or not. What's it gonna be?"

"We'll take it." This time Annie was quick enough to jump in before Mary. "I'm bored and besides, we can always check it with Mike straight after." Annie found herself standing between the two older girls. She didn't think either would throw a punch, not without a reason, but she still felt compelled to keep them apart.

"Annie, you know how Thomas came into The Hopper last night?"

Annie and Mary exchanged glances. "Sure."

"He's got sumpin' on him that Mike wants back. Keeps it in his wallet in his breast pocket."

"What is it?"

"It's a secret. Mike wants it nicked. That's all ya need to know."

"Sounds like a rum deal." Mary's face was starting to look sour, like she'd bit into a lump of bad potato.

"Why us?" Annie interjected.

The sneer flashed across Ida's face again like it had never left, only been hiding behind the smile. "'Cos he don't know you two. Mary's the best pickpocket outta the kiddos and Annie's not got a reputation yet." She made a point of starting Annie right in the eyes when she spoke. Annie made a point of not looking away. She didn't have to now, not after the brick thrown the day before.

"Why not you?"

"Thomas knows me, he knows I hang around the Hopper and the Gophers. He ain't gonna trust me any further than he gotta."

Mary opened her mouth to interject, but Ida held up a finger to stop her. "An' don't ask about Trick, he's down at the docks waiting for the Water Sow to come in. Besides, Thomas has a thing for ladies, don't trust the lads."

That satisfied Mary. Maybe not every little detail, but the fact that Ida had an actual reason for choosing them made a difference. It meant she weren't sending them off to get into trouble, or to stay out of something interesting.

"So, we just need the wallet?" Mary continued her questions. She had a list, Annie knew, things you always asked before a job. Annie could only ever remember a few of them, but she was working on it.

"Yep an' no. You hafta get the wallet, get the paper, then put the wallet back."

"Aw geez."

"We don't want Thomas to know it's gone straightaway. Don't take nothin' else. That's why Mike's givin' the marker. He knows this is troublesome, and he wants ta make extra sure nobody gets greedy." Ida shook a finger, like getting greedy was something any one of the Gophers could avoid.

"I hate ya, ye know that, right?" Mary seemed caught between annoyance at Ida for not being up-front about the difficulty of the trick and pride at being tasked with something hard to do.

"What's on tha paper?" Annie asked.

"Not yer bisness. Mike sez it's got spellstuff all over it, so you'll prolly get turned into a frog if you even look at it cross-eyed."

"Then how are we gonna know we got the right paper?"

"If there's more than one, just bring 'em all." Ida snapped. "Mary, you lift the wallet, pass it to Annie so she can get ta paper, then she can pass it back to you. If he does notice it's gone, he won't find it on ye."

"Fine, how quick?"

"Quick as ye can."

The conversation was interrupted by a young man with bright blue eyes and red hair cut so close it looked like the fuzz on a peach.

"Oi, Ida."

"Oi, Ginger." Ida's attitude had gone from imperious to coquette in less time than it took to blink. Ginger put his hands on her shoulders and tried to place a kiss on her bare neck. Mary and Annie looked askance at one another, Mary amused, Annie horrified.

"What's ye friends upta then?" He didn't actually look at either of the younger girls, his attention entirely on Ida.

"Leavin'." Ida answered shortly. Mary was a little quicker on the uptake and she grabbed Annie's arm, the two girls bolting from the courtyard and giggling as they ran.

FOUR

"Why canna we just wait 'til he's drunk himself into a gutter somewhere, then take his wallet?" It seemed like a much simpler solution to Annie. Mary never did anything halfway, she'd sent three of the littlest kids to go scout out Thomas' recent hangouts and they'd reported back in record time. One of the drawbacks of being a conman, Annie supposed, being easy to find was part of the deal.

"Guy like Shy Thomas' been rolled more times than we got years combined," Mary pointed out. "Once he gits ta drinkin' we'll hafta stand in line just to give him a wink."

"So we gotta hit him up before he hits the saloons?"

"Ayup."

"Ain't that harder?" Annie was all thumbs. She was quick on her feet, but emptying pockets, other than her own, was something she'd never quite gotten the hang of. Mary kept on trying to teach her, and Annie kept on trying to learn, but they'd taken a break after Annie'd ripped the pocket right out of Mary's coat trying to lift out a small bag of rocks. Mary'd said coins were better to practice with because they clinked if you messed up and, if you had coins to practice with, it meant you could get a sweet roll from the street vendors when you were tired of practicing.

"Depends on Thomas." The two girls were seated on a low wall, just up the street from where Thomas was chatting up a couple of the younger, prettier fruit sellers. "I can't get at him in any of the regular places, he's too pretty and there's too much competition."

Ma always said to judge a man by his shoes. *A nice coat's easy to nick, but if he's got nice shoes that fit right, you're looking at a man with means.* Thomas' shoes were badly patched and in need of a polish. Annie held up a thumb to block the sight of the lower half of him. From the hips up he was as fine a gent as she'd ever laid eyes on. Black hair carefully swept back, clean shaven, starched collar and pressed coat without any holes or wear around the edges. Ma was a seamstress, she'd lectured at Annie for hours about how clothes went together and came apart over time and how to fix or avoid the damage. You tried to never do repairs for a customer, only for the family. You wanted the clients to ask for new ones, then you could take the old castoffs and remake them to sell or use yourself.

"How about the Trolley?"

"HA." Mary's laugh had no fun in it. "The trolley's all fingers these days. You start with a coin in yer pocket at one end and by the time you've got to the back that coin has passed through every pair of fingers and back into yer own pocket, if you're lucky. No one's e'er that lucky." The older girl waggled her fingers expectantly, as if warming up.

"Ye got the right idea though." Mary admitted. "We need something along those lines, someplace crowded, someplace he goes, regular like. Someplace he feels safe enough to hang his coat up maybe."

"How about the Dens?" Nice girls weren't supposed to know about the mystic smoke of the ash dens and places where crooks went to find men to strip, both of clothing and virtue, but Annie heard enough from the grandmothers around the washbin to know about such places.

Mary laughed out loud this time. "Geez, Annie. You mean the whorehouses?" Annie winced inside at the words, but kept a straight face on top of it. "Every time I think yer a proper Starchie, you go and drop something like that one. Ya gotta use the right words though, or people will think yer not ta be trusted, got it?"

Annie nodded. "Whorehouses." She said out loud. Her ears turned red from the thought of the boxing Ma'd give them for even hinting the word out loud. "If he takes the coat off, we can get at it, right?"

"Yeah, but it's the same problem as the trolley. Every gal with light fingers stops by there lookin' for a stupid lad, and I don't think Thomas is stupid enough to get taken on those grounds."

Returning the wallet meant a lot more planning had to be done. Annie understood now why Ida had come to Mary. Mary was patient, Mary was careful. She stalked her mark and emptied his pockets when everything was to her advantage. Sometimes she waited too long and someone with faster fingers got in first, but Annie knew that anyone who took one of Mary's marks didn't keep their ill-gotten gains for long. It wasn't common knowledge yet, but Mary was becoming a force to be reckoned with.

It also meant there was a lot of sitting and watching, which was Annie's least favorite thing in the world.

A lady, Ma said, *ought to be able to sit for an hour without budging an eyelash*. Annie grinned at the thought of using all that sitting for something useful, other than looking like a fancied up coatrack.

"What's that face fer?"

"Ma used to make us practice sitting and waiting. Bet she never thought it would come in handy for nickin' stuff."

"Bein' patient keeps ye from gettin' caught." Mary replied with all seriousness. A nudge brought Annie's attention back over to Thomas who had finished charming the fruit girl out of an orange.

"C'mon, he's gonna move." Mary cast a disparaging glance at the black-haired girl across the street. "She's gonna catch holy whatfor when her ma finds out she gave away a whole orange like that."

"Why'd she give it to him then?"

"Some girls like boys too much, their heads get all addled when they get close up." Mary sneered as they hopped off the wall and headed down the street to the corner.

"Ya think Ida's one of those?"

"What, you mean about Ginger this mornin? Nah, Ida's all business. Whatever she's got goin' on with Ginger, she's got a plan." Mary spat. "Won't catch that one getting tossed over by any boy, not unless there's a way ta come out ahead." They arrived at the corner well ahead of Thomas and turned, ambling a few paces further down before pausing and putting their backs casually up against the wall.

"What if Thomas goes back the other direction?"

"Has he backtracked at all today? Guys like Thomas, they go forward, always forward. They have a THING about goin' back o'er their own feetsteps. Besides, if that gal's Ma is there when he passes by again, she's going to make it a twofer and beat the stuffing out of him just like she will her own kid."

True to Mary's prediction, Thomas continued his ambling pace, up the street and past the girls. Every so often he'd stop and talk. Sometimes with a shop owner, sometimes to the indigent souls that sat along the wall, feet drawn up and cups or bowls at the ready.

"What's he doin' anyways." Annie had never seen a man with so much time to waste talking. *He had to be GOING somewhere, didn't he?*

"Glad-handing." Mary answered offhandedly. "Watch close, sometimes you can see him pass a coin when he shakes a hand." She stared openly for a moment, then shook her head. "He's really good, I heard he used to be a pickpocket before he got hisself a fancy coat."

"That's a lot o' coins."

"Nah, he ain't given one ta everybody, but he's makin' sure they all know who he is and they think nice things when his name comes up."

"So he's buyin' friends."

"Goodwill maybe, I dunno if you'd say "friend", but they'll be happy to tell the King's Guard they ain't seen him fer days if it comes up, or they might let him know when the butcher's mistress comes to call. If he paid 'm every time they start expecting it. This way he keeps them paying attention."

"Bits and pieces of friend-stuff then. Why?"

Mary gave her a condescending look. "Ye ask too damn many questions, ye know that? That's just what guys like Thomas do. They're too skinny ta throw a good punch, too finicky ta get blood on their shirts, they hate traveling so they don't go out adventurin'. They make their way by talkin' people inta doin' stuff an' getting others ta take the punches for it."

Thomas' saunter had brought him to the front of a dingy-windowed shop with a bright blue door.

"Oh really?" Mary grabbed Annie's wrist. They stayed put just long enough for Thomas to greet someone inside the door, then disappear into the offices. "Ya see that?"

"Defender's office?"

"Geez, I told you not to let on that ye ken read."

"So?" Annie wasn't about to be put off this time. Something new was afoot.

"That's Dayton Landry's offices."

Most of the defenders Annie was familiar with spent their time hanging around near the bars and dens, waiting for a raid by the King's Guard or a bar brawl to toss a few clients their way. Offices were for defenders whose clients came to find them instead.

"Why's he goin' in there? He ain't in trouble right now, is he?" Annie kept up with the questions.

"Dunno yet." The wait was longer than even the long-experienced Mary could stand.

"Go see what he's upta." Annie nudged Mary.

"Hmph." The sun was passing right overhead, the grime from the street passing upwards into streamers of fairy-dust. Annie pressed herself back against the wall to try and keep the sun from pounding on the top of her head, but the shadow had long since given up and gone away. Mary didn't budge. Instead, she rummaged around in her skirts and produced a clove-studded apple.

"Why not? Did he go out the back maybe?" Annie watched, fascinated, as Mary turned the apple over in her grimy fingertips, plucking each clove and collecting them into her palm.

"He did'na go out the back."

"So why's he still in there?"

Mary idly returned the handful of nubs to her pocket, then wiped the sticky residue on her throat and the back of her neck. The sweet pungency reached Annie's nose even over the stink of the streets. The older girl bounced the apple on her palm.

"I think he's s'posed ta be there." Mary reached out a hand and snagged the shirt of one of the ever-underfoot street urchins. He was probably an underfed six years, barefoot and begrimed. Mary waggled the apple under his nose.

"Wots yer name, kiddo?"

He sized her up, brown eyes older than the rest of his face.

"Bertrand. Wotcha want?"

Mary flipped the apple into the air and caught it deftly on the back of her hand, then rolled it back over into her palm again. His eyes followed the motion with a greed borne from equal parts need and want. He clearly knew the drill, even a kid just a couple years older than Tate.

"See that shop over there? The one with the blue door?"

"Yeah?"

"I need ya ta take a peek inside and tell me if ye see a guy with yella hair and a green waistcoat in there."

"Want me ta nick sumpin'?"

"No."

"Break sumpin'?"

"No."

"Gots it. Then what?" He hooked his thumbs into the bit of rope that held his pants up.

"Meet us on the corner over there, got it?" Mary nodded in the direction the street ended. You didn't ever point, looked suspicious.

"You betcha." He scampered into the street, dodging in between passers-by. Annie winced as he ducked around one of the plate-footed drays that hauled carts of dry goods up from the docks. The horse barely even flicked an ear as it concentrated on placing one slow foot in front of the other.

"C'mon, this way." Mary led Annie in the opposite direction, away from their cozy spot by the wall and towards the end of the street.

Around the corner, the boy was waiting, thumbs hooked under his armpits, mimicking a grown man's braces.

"Oi." Mary sidled up to him on one side, Annie took the other. They looked for all the world like three sibs waiting on a fourth.

"Oi! That fella that chased me out, he's the one yer lookin' for, right?"

"Yep."

"He was at a desk writin' letters. Tiny desk, his knees were all bunched up under it."

Mary used a few colorful words that reddened Annie's ears and drew a smirk from the boy.

"Was his coat at the desk?"

"Nah, no room. There's a coat-rack at the back. Everyone's in shirt-sleeves and it smells like tar and old farts in there. Some old guy in the corner keeps givin' everyone the evil eye. I don't think they woulda even noticed me going in there, 'cept for that one guy gettin' all shouty."

"Thanks." Mary tossed him the apple and it vanished from the air. Annie didn't see where it went, but the boy jammed his hands into his pockets and sauntered off.

"So now what?"

Mary tossed her that look, the one that meant that Annie had asked a silly question again. She didn't say a word, just sauntered on down the street. Annie heaved an exasperated sigh and followed her.

Mary led the way down one alleyway and up another. The

space between the buildings here was cold and dank, the sun never threw more than a few beams of light down here. The alleys on this side were warmed only by the actions of the businesses and the bums who scavenged through the dustbins. In the winter that meant extra work, but now, in the heat of summer it meant a cool escape, stink notwithstanding. Nobody batted an eye at an extra pair of kids trying to get out of the day's heat and nobody looked up when Mary quietly led her further in, counting doors as they went. The backs of the buildings were all the same weathered grey wood and stained red brick. The doors stood at different heights off the ground, some had steps, some not, but had all been painted with the same brush. All the bits that made one storefront look different from another were saved for the front of the building, the parts people could see. Annie didn't think they had any chance of finding the right door, but she followed Mary anyway.

The older girl stopped abruptly, examining a pair of fairly well-matched doorways. The bottom of both stood at knee height from the ground, both painted the same faded green, both looked to Annie's inexperienced eyes like they were locked from the inside.

"Which one is it?"

"Shut it, I'm doin' numbers to figger out which." Mary buried her hands in her skirts, tugging and shifting until Annie heard a solid metal thump as something hit the ground. "Grab that, willya?" Mary took three great steps over to the third door, cupping a hand and putting an ear to the crack where it met the lintel. Neither door had a handle, or any obvious way to get them open.

That turned out to be an iron bar the length of Annie's forearm. The ends were pinched flat like the ones they used down at the docks for opening crates. It was heavier than it looked, colder than it should have been for something tucked away next to the skin.

Mary moved to the second door, then waved Annie over.

"What are you doing with a pry bar in your pockets?"

"Opening doors, silly." She deftly slipped the narrow end of the bar under the corner of the door and gave it a twist. The motion popped the door upwards, slipped the latch and pulled the door open just enough for Annie to get her fingertips around the edge. From there it was just a quiet, quick tug and Mary slipped out of sight inside, leaving Annie holding the prybar.

Annie used the toe of her boot to keep the door open just a crack. The warm air from the inside trickled out into an alley that felt eerily silent. She counted off the seconds.

"Psst." The edge of a man's wallet peeked out through the doorway. Annie stared at it suspiciously. It had once been a fine thing but the crispness of the leatherwork had been worn down by fingertips and time, the wards of protection blurred until their power was lost.

The wallet bounced up and down impatiently, making Annie miss her first grab at it. She had to lean the pry-bar against the wall, holding it there with knees and skirts while she thumbed through the contents. The leather was soft under her fingertips, the silk lining ripped and stained. She found what she was looking for folded into the space usually reserved for bills. A bit of paper folded over twice and stained red where the sealing wax had been picked off. As the light struck it, there was a flash, a matched pair of black lines, like elevens finger-painted in charcoal, appeared on the paper, then vanished as it moved into shadow. Annie didn't recognize the mark, but she knew it wasn't proper lettering. It made her uncomfortable, even thinking about it made her fingertips prickle with distaste. The spellstuff Ida had warned about, Annie reasoned. She pulled the packet out and tucked it away into her sleeve, keeping it well away from her skin, before slipping the wallet back through the crack in the door. It was nipped from her fingertips straightaway and Annie stifled a sigh of relief. Even if Mary was caught now, she could plead off, Annie had the paper and was already headed back down the alley at a brisk walk.

She hesitated a bit over the pry bar, it seemed to get heavier with every step. Mary would give her holy whatfor if she left it behind, so she hung onto it, holding it against her right side, buried in her skirts. She might come out of it with a bruised shin but that was better than Mary's shouting and carrying-on.

You didn't walk too fast or too slow when you were *upta sumpin'*, but it took all of Annie's concentration to keep from bolting. It was the eyes. It felt like everybody's eyes were on you. Like everybody knew exactly what you had done from the expression on your face and the spring in your step.

She listened for the sound of the door behind her, but the noise and bustle from the street had returned and she could not make anything out. The heat of the summer sun hit like a wave when she exited the alley, it put a stutter in her step. She turned and continued walking, rejoining the bustle of activity and disappearing, just another grimy face in the crowd.

FIVE

The guilt was the most surprising part. It was part of the plan, the plan she and Mary and had put together. Annie could not shake the feeling that she had abandoned her friend. As she counted her steps to their meeting place she fought the urge to go back to see if Mary had been caught.

"Stick to the plan" she reminded herself. "Mary's just fine. She'll meet you at the Promenade."

She wondered if this was normal, this worry that gnawed in the pit of her stomach. Mary never seemed to worry, nor did Ida or Dutch or any of the other kids she ran with. She didn't dare ask them, didn't dare ask any of them just in case it was only her. She supposed it was the kind of thing you grew into, like her older brother Marco's ears. Maybe there was a magic number, after you've pulled ten jobs you stop being quite so nervous. Either way she decided she didn't want to work with anything else using a prybar. It kept banging her ankles as she walked down the street.

The Promenade wasn't nearly as fancy as it sounded. A whole row of houses had burned themselves down to foundations.

Declaring it an "eyesore", the Moonlight Ladies Auxiliary had come up with a beautification plan to turn it into a park with trees and flower boxes. Where the Starchies gathered, money followed, and in short order the area around the park had been overrun with pop up stalls selling all manner of goods and comestibles. After a few dust-ups with the King's Guard, because you couldn't build anything new without having to placate the King's Guard, a sort of truce had been declared. The sellers of goods took over the lanes surrounding the park and any bare patches within. The Starchies still had their greenswards and rose borders dotted with shade trees. Every so often you'd get a scuffle as one vendor tried to take over the coveted patch of dirt that was six inches closer to the shade, but Mary often pointed it out as a near-perfect balance of enterprising hustlers and well-monied layabouts. This late in the day it would be filled with people looking to escape the baking heat of the offices and apartments, two more girls in the mix would go unnoticed.

Annie slowed down and stuck to the far edge of the sidewalk, peering down each cross street to catch the tops of the trees that marked the Promenade.

"Oi, miss, lookin fer sumpin?" The boy that skipped up and matched pace with her was no one she recognized. Slightly less grubby, shirtsleeves rolled up, feet bare with too many toes, his first impression made Annie resist the urge to clutch at the note hidden in her sleeve. Untrustworthy, the twinkle in his too-big eyes said. Aelfheid maybe, one of the loners that came to High Charity looking for adventure or work or whatever. She could have kicked herself. Looking for the right street must have drawn his attention. She'd looked lost, which was almost as bad as looking *upta sumpin'*.

"Meetin' my Da." She answered shortly and quickened her pace. Something about this boy smelled like trouble. Something said he was looking for trouble.

"What's your Da needing the prybar for?"

Annie's spark of elation that her lie had held up was quickly replaced by the realization that she would have to tell an even bigger one.

"I dinna ask. He says get the bar, I get the bar." She mumbled a bit, retreated into herself. Plenty of kids fetched and carried for the grownups, maybe he'd leave her alone if he thought her Da was a beast.

"Aaight, but tell yer da that he's in Spitter territory. If he's doing anything shady, he's gonna catch hell."

Annie opened her mouth to retort that it certainly was NOT Spitter territory, but bit her tongue before the words got out. She nodded instead, dropping her eyes to her boot tops. When she looked up again, the boy was closer, leaning in. He was just half a head taller than she, and his presence suddenly felt smothering.

Onions again. Everybody seemed to be eating onions this week.

She considered dropping the prybar on his toes but any sort of physical response would simply get him to chase her. It was the kind of thing she could've gotten away with if she was a little bit younger, a little more wee. Stomping on toes and kicking shins were children's insults. She was not a child. She had brought the bakery cart to a standstill by sheer force of will and one fist-sized brick.

"Da's waitin'," she said simply and ducked around him. There was a good chance he wouldn't grab her here out in the middle of the street. If he did she'd have to create a scene which wouldn't help at all. The specter of a brutal father must've done it's work because he let her scamper on past.

She didn't use any of Ma's list of unladylike words out loud, but she ran through them all in her head, twice. That brief encounter meant that she couldn't go straightaways to meet Mary. She was going to go have to go around, maybe stash the prybar while she was at it.

Annie kept up her businesslike pace, still looking for the Promenade with quick glances down every side street, but her mind was racing. She had to find a way to loop back around to Mary without bringing any trouble with her.

While her feet kept her moving forward, her mind reviewed all the stories Mary'd ever told her about clever escapes and sneaky hiding places. Most of them involved a lot of running. She didn't mind the running, but it would draw attention and maybe make things even worse. She spotted the green of the treetops that marked the Promenade, and made a note of the blue-fronted bakery on the corner. When she came back, she'd be able to find the street without so much looking about.

Knowing where she was going eased her mind a bit. All the looking about let her know that whoever the Aelfheid boy was, he was still keeping tabs on her. He wasn't very good at it. Probably could've used some lessons from Mary. Annie kept her eyes open and picked a shop she recognized across the street. The doors stood open against the heat of the day so she was able to duck inside without causing a fuss.

"Hallo, Annie, are you looking for Mick?" The woman behind the counter was a head and a half taller than Annie's own Ma. The shop was filled with bolts and bolts of fabric stacked from the floor to the ceiling. Mick did the deliveries, carrying boxes of shirts and dresses across the city. He used to be one of the Gophers before he went legit. By hiring a former Gopher the shop retained some immunity from the activities of the group. It didn't keep Mick from catching a beating for getting an address wrong, but it meant that mixups were usually just that, mixups.

"Thanks Miss Ellen." Lots of the kiddo Gophers didn't believe in pleases or thank you's but Annie found it made grownups so much easier to deal with. She skipped through the door with the back of the shop and popped up the stairs to where Mick was sorting his deliveries into paper boxes and rolls.

"Hey, Annie what're you up to?" Mick never seemed surprised, never surprised by anything, in fact. He just kept quietly folding cut swatches of fabric into tissue paper wrapped bundles. Annie showed him the prybar.

"Can I stash this here for an hour? It's too heavy and I have to get across town."

He grinned. "As long as you didn't bash in a head with it." A year in the shop had taken the edge off his words, the street patois Annie was used to hearing all day had started to fill out with fewer dropped sounds. He glanced down the length of the bar as if to be sure she'd cleaned it properly, then slipped it neatly into a gap between two of the bolts of fabric that lined the walls.

"Thanks, you're a sweetie." Annie didn't wait for his response, she turned and took the steps two at a time down to the back exit and the ever-present alleyway. She popped her head out of the doorway first and took a careful look. The back of the shop directly opposite had its door standing open to help dissolve the summer's heat. It only took any half a dozen steps to cross the alleyway into the other shop and another dozen or so to skip around the patrons inside and out the front door. The Promenade was tantalizingly close. She could see the tops of the trees over the buildings. It was much easier to walk casually now that she wasn't trying to conceal the prybar and she reached the near edge of the Promenade without any other incident.

The trees beckoned, tops waving slightly in a breeze that never made it down between the buildings. Sellers had parked their carts all along the cobbled walkway that encircled the park, making the already hot summer air thick with the smell of grease. Cold things were on offer as well, sliced meats and cold sausages, beer pumped from a portable tap and shaved ice that she'd never tried, not even once. Her stomach rumbled and she resolutely marched into the patches of shade. She had no coins and the lump of porridge had long since been digested. She could head home to get a bite to eat after she met with Mary. If she was really lucky Mary might have another plan, something that might score a few pennies or a slice of bread. Annie would have considered handing the paper over to Ida in exchange for slice of meat or a handful of peanuts. *That*, she decided, *is the real problem with working for favors*. Favors didn't fill a belly either.

The Promenade always seemed like a strange place to Annie. Elsewhere in the city people dodged one another, filled the sidewalks to stay out of the offal in the gutters. Here in the promenade, even on days that were really hot and shade was hard to come by, everyone maintained a certain space between themselves. For a child used to ducking and darting in and out of foot traffic, the Promenade was a breeze to travel along.

"Oi, Annie, what took ya so long?" Mary appeared at her elbow and the younger girl jumped, startled.

"Cripes, Mary, warn a girl next time," said Annie once she'd recovered.

"Shoulda been looking." Mary grinned, flush with their success.

"Oh, here ..." Annie reached into her sleeve for the Note but

Mary shook her head.

"No, no. Keep it hid. If Ida pulls something funny, she's gonna come after me ta git that, not you."

Annie frowned. She didn't like to think Ida would try to cheat them out of their reward, it wasn't fair. Ida could be mean, but Annie couldn't remember her being a cheat about anything.

"Now," Mary said, rubbing her hands together. "There's a new guy on the corner selling sweet rolls. He's had a bit of a nip, might not be awake all that long, if you know what I mean."

Annie nodded. After all, she was on a roll now, two capers under her belt, might as well go for three.

SIX

Annie's tummy wasn't full, but it had stopped complaining. Mary had been quicker, snatching a bun in each hand before bolting. Annie had tried to do the same when the seller had turned to shout, but she'd missed and came away with only a single, much smaller roll of her own.

Didn't matter. She told herself. It was all her own. This time she felt a pang of guilt. This wasn't a task set to her, a job to be done. This was just taking something for herself. This felt much more like stealing. The joy of success felt hollow, especially since she could have simply gone home and begged a meal from Ma. Mary didn't have such a luxury. Maybe that was why she was so good at stealing things. Maybe she was better at it because she had to be.

"Oi, whatcha so worried about?" Mary had gotten ahead of Annie by a few paces. Now she slowed down. The Promenade was a few streets behind them and the sun still remained stubbornly overhead, shining light into all the city's corners.

"Just Starchie stuff," Annie said haughtily and flipped her braid back over her shoulder.

"Oh it's gonna be like that, is it! C'mon now, whatcha thinkin' about?"

"You don't really think Ida's going to try and cheat us, do ya?"

"Course I do. I think everybody's gonna try and cheat us if we give 'em the chance. But Ida, well Ida's got plans. She wants ta be a force, someone who gets the menfolk ta do her bidding. Anyone who got plans in this town is someone you gotta watch out for."

Annie was quiet for a few minutes as they dodged the slower foot traffic.

"Is that why you and Ida don't get along? She's got aspirations and you think she's gonna cheat to get what she wants?"

"Nah. It's worse than that."

Annie waited for the good part of the story to start, but Mary remained silent. It seemed that was all she had to say on the matter.

"Hey, is it true the Spitters took over the street by the dress shop?" Annie picked a new topic. They had another few blocks to walk and talking kept her mind off the blisters her too big shoes were starting.

It worked, Mary gave her a shocked look. "Where'd you hear a fool thing like that? 'Course not! Spitters taking over one o' our streets? They got no balls fer a fight."

The boundaries shifted from time to time, Annie knew, but she didn't know how they changed hands, outside of a bloody brawl. There were streets in contention too, she knew enough to stay away from those.

She relayed the encounter with the barefoot boy to Mary.

"Whaddya mean you ditched mah prybar!" Mary flushed red, completely missing the point of the story.

"It's safe, I just gotta go pick it up."

"You weren't supposed ta go stomping around wit it slung over yer shoulder." Mary griped.

"There's no way I can hide that thing under my skirt, I don't have the pockets you do." Annie countered tartly. "I stashed it someplace safe with someone we can trust. We can go back and get it after we take the note to Ida."

The folded paper was light, she couldn't feel it tucked up in her sleeve unless she shifted her elbow around. Still, it weighed on a corner of her mind, she couldn't forget it was there.

"Ya don't use pockets fer something like that, ya gotta twist it up in yer petticoat, otherwise it'll rip right out ta bottom." Mary said grumpily.

"Fine, we can go back and get it as soon as we get this thing to Ida."

"In a hurry, are ya?"

"Yeah. If Ida's gonna cheat us like you think, I think we ought to get it over with quick."

Mary punched her friend lightly in the shoulder with a laugh. "See, now yer thinkin' makes some sense." Annie kept pace as the sidewalk changed from cobbles to wood. The sidewalks were put there in an attempt to escape the mud and muck of the streets in winter. In summer, the dogs that ran loose would dig underneath to hide from the sun. They stayed absolutely silent even with feet stomping overhead. Annie amused herself by trying to catch a glimpse of fur from between the slats as they walked.

"Whaddya thinkin' on the paper." Annie finally asked by way of restarting the conversation. Mary took a few seconds to answer and when she did she kept her voice low, like she was worried about being overheard.

"It's gotta be blackmail. Dirty letters, maybe sumpin'

somebody never shoulda written down. That's why I don't trust writing, y'know. Whatever it is, it's gotta be important."

"Shouldn't we take a look at it? I mean, shouldn't we make sure we got the right piece of paper?" Annie's heart clenched at the idea that they might have gone to all that trouble for nothing. They might have made hash of the entire assignment. The thought brought her to a stop on the already bustling sidewalk and she resisted the urge to paw through her sleeves to find the Note.

"Geez, Annie." Mary reached back and grabbed her arm to drag her along. "What goes on in that Starchie skull o' yours? Course we got the right one. Wasn't anything else in the wallet was there?"

"Maybe it was the wrong wallet."

"Oh Jesus, you've got tha willies, that's whatcha got."

"The what?"

"Willies. Sometimes people get stupid. The idea gets in their head that they nicked the wrong thing, or someone made 'em on the way out o' ta building." Mary elaborated and increased her pace. "That's the kinda thing that gits ya caught. Ya get an idea in yer head, then ya do sumpin' stupid like go back to see if you dropped a pin or walk past the mark ya just skimmed ta see if he's noticed yet."

"So how do you fix that?" Annie asked.

"It's kinda like remembering to brush yer hair. You keep doing it till you feel funny when ye fergit. Ye gotta remember ta never, ever look back."

"So you're sure..." Annie began, stubbornly, unable to shake the creeping feeling.

"Absolutely. Being worried about Ida is just good sense because she's stuck me with a bum gig before. This is just fanciful stuff in yer head. Ignore that stuff."

"Hey, you!"

It was a man's voice that interrupted Mary's impromptu lesson. An angry man's voice. Mary didn't bother to look, she just bolted. Annie jumped to the side, out of the way of the very angry fishmonger that charged past. The smell of eels lingered in his wake. Annie could hear Mary laughing as she hotfooted it down the street. Annie knew what was coming next and she changed her own path, turning to skip across traffic. The move required dodging carts and hooves, so most of the time grownups pulled up short instead of giving chase. Whoever the Fishmonger was, he would come after Annie after Mary ditched him. Annie wasn't in the mood to be cuffed or shaken.

She was brought up short by hand on the back of her collar.

"Not so fast Missy."

She froze, some combination of calculation and panic. She recognized the voice from earlier. The boy who warned her off the street now had a firm grip at the back of her neck. She'd been so focused on getting away she'd missed the Fishmonger's accomplice.

"I warned you this was Spitter territory. Bobby's going to grab your little friend and we're going to have a little chat about staying in your own neighborhood."

"Ain't Spitter territory." Annie was scared, and mad. Mad that she was shaking like a leaf. Mad that she'd been caught. Mad that the summer sun had been making her underthings all sticky. Mad that this boy was going to humiliate her and Mary by making an example outta them.

Annie spun on her heel and let him have it with a fist in the face. It was like punching the hind end of a mule. Her hand hurt, her knuckles stung and the jackass on the other end looked like he hadn't felt a thing.

"Knock it off." He stepped back, trying to stay out of range.

Annie kept her right arm free and used it to hammer at his shoulders, trying for another shot at his face. As long as he had a grip on her dress she was stuck, it wasn't something she could just shimmy out of. She wiggled in his grip, trying to shake loose. He was only a head taller, but it gave him the advantage. He lifted upward, pulling her off the ground. Without purchase, Annie couldn't pivot, couldn't turn to get a proper swing at him. Worse yet, he was laughing now, a high-pitched snort that just made her more angry.

It was bad enough she had to smile and duck swings and torments from Ma in her own home, but out here on the streets it was intolerable. Everybody could see, everybody could laugh at her powerlessness.

She jammed a hand into her pocket, the pull of his fist on her dress bringing the object of desire closer to her hand. It was a short, sharp piece of brick, wedge shaped and cold, despite the long heat of the day. She gave up trying to reach the ground and abruptly yanked her knees upward, putting the weight of a thirteen-year-old girl and a full set of petticoats to work for her.

"Hey now, you're not getting away that easy". He laughed and reached to grab her arm. His grip sagged and she brought her feet back onto the ground, using the momentum to spin again. Her outstretched arm was just barely short, but the extra three inches granted by the brickbat in her grip made contact. He had been expecting another ineffectual punch. Instead the broken edges cut parallel lines across his face, from the ear to the nose. Bright blood blossomed in the wake of her attack. He cursed and dropped Annie, both hands up to protect his outsized eyes from the snarling mass of girl he was now faced with. He hadn't been expecting a real fight.

She started running as soon as she saw his hands, the dress still bunched up behind her shoulders. It felt like he still had a grip on her so she ducked one way, then the other to be sure she was free. She lowered her shoulders as she ran so that if anyone did make a grab for her, she'd be moving too fast to be stopped. She didn't think anyone else would get involved, but she'd misjudged once already. She didn't want to get grabbed again. Mary'd never let her hear the end of it.

SEVEN

"Ma." Annie started carefully, trying to judge the woman's mood before going too far.

Ma was at her sewing table, a plank of wood that stretched from the windowsill to the back of the old wooden chest. She had her whole kit out, threads and buttons and symbols and snippets of fine fabric left over from repairs and resizes. It was a good sign. Ma was always happiest when she was sewing.

"Yes, Annie." The older woman matched the edges of the fabric together, face-to-face and pinned them into place with nary a tremble in her fingertips.

"Ma, I saw a symbol today. It wasn't a letter like for reading and writing. One of the other girls said it was spellstuff, I didn't think so." Annie spoke carefully, making sure she used Ma's favored pronunciations.

"Did you get in a fight about it?" Ma spared her a glance, the watery blue eyes as sharp as the pins in the fabric.

"We disagreed." Annie said. *Ladies didn't fight*, Ma had told her over and over. Annie knew better than to make up a story with a fight in it. "But if I was wrong, I ought to own up to it, right?"

Ma sighed with the patience of a parent who'd not yet hit the bottle. "What didja see, then?"

"Two lines come up and down like elevens, but thick, like painting with your fingers, and they curve out just a bit at the bottom."

"Sounds like a lazy-made eleven to me. What made your friend think it wasn't?"

Annie kept herself from shrugging, another low gesture on a long list that Ma couldn't abide.

"It wasn't all there. It kind of looked like a charcoal mark, but you could only see it when it was in a shadow."

"Your friend's right." Ma pointed the sharp end of the scissors at Annie. "That weren't a letter. That's a sigil. That's Tok, may the Moonlight keep him from the streets of High Charity." Ma pressed a thumb into the space between her eyebrows, the pressure leaving a little white moon behind for a few seconds. A chill ran down Annie's spine. It had been years and years since she'd seen Ma invoke the Moonlight.

"Which one's Tok?" Annie asked. It seemed Ma was in a talking mood and it would be a shame to waste it.

"Sit." Mom pointed at the floor. "You can sort the bobbins while I remind you."

Annie settled her skirts on the floor around her and pulled the box of bobbins closer. Tate and his friend Millie had been playing in them again, pretending the bright colored threads wound onto spools of golden wood were a treasure to be hoarded.

"Back when I were still in the service of our Lady, we had a wizard come through town. High Charity was smaller then. We didn't have the Highwall. The Promenade where you hang out with your friends was still mostly bog, full of bog-fae. They used to sell mud crabs at the market once a week."

"I don't think I've ever met a bog-fae?"

"You wouldn't, they left when we drained the bog. This wizard, name of… Aldus? Aurix? Pretty short name for a wizard, but he was looking for a messenger of Tok and he was looking for Moonlight's help."

"Why would the Acolytes help out a wizard?" Annie wanted to know. Ma's stories could get fantastic, but wizards were rare, even ones with names too short.

"Well, you know the hierarchies, right? Each Kingship has its pantheon, each city represents one of those spirits. What most folk don't know is they're all connected. The Lady in Moonlight has a pair of twins under her charge. Tok and Sho. Tok's an agent of chaos, breaking down and causing failures over time. Sho is also an agent of chaos, the kind that makes new things happen, mixes up the order, breaks the rules for the better. You can't have one without the other, but they don't get along very well. They tend to cancel each other out. A spirit like Tok is always trying to find a foothold someplace where Sho don't have a presence yet.

"So the Agent of Tok was upta sumpin'?" Annie asked. *Upta sumpin'* Annie could understand. *Upta sumpin'* was Gopher territory.

"Up TO something." Ma corrected sharply.

"Sorry Ma, up TO something." Annie repeated herself, saying the words clearly and crisply. She continued to sort the bobbins, re-rolling the threads that needed it, placing each in its socket in the bottom of the box.

Ma's gaze softened. "But yes, the Agent of Tok was here to bring Tok's influence into High Charity. The wizard and one of the

Acolytes found him and turned him over to the King's Guard."

"Were you the Acolyte?"

Ma's eyes darkened. Annie could swear she could still see the ghost of a moon in the space between her mother's eyes.

"Sorry, Ma, wasn't trying to pry." Annie ducked her head in submission. The topic of Ma's leaving the order was taboo. Annie knew that Ma fell afoul of an order from Lady Moonlight herself, but everything else remained unsaid.

"The problem with Tok," Ma pointed the long sharp blades of the scissors at Annie again. "Is he uses people to do his works. Not avatars, not like when the Lady possesses an Acolyte to walk the city and still possesses a portion of her Moonlight power. You KNOW when the Lady is present. Instead, Tok stays in the shadows, he inspires the worst in us. If Tok has influence in a town, you must be on your guard against your own self." Ma snipped the ends of a loose thread for emphasis. "And that is one of the most difficult things you can ask a person to do."

Annie held up the last bobbin. It was her favorite. She'd never seen Ma use the thread, a fine gauge that was hard to see as a single strand, but wound around the wooden bobbin it became a luminous, unearthly white.

"All right. Off with you. And if you see Tok's mark again, stay well away from it, you hear?"

"Yes, Ma."

"Go collect Toby from Kimberbokker's place and keep him busy until supper. I have to finish this mending before nightfall."

"Yes, Ma."

Getting the crowbar back to Mary would have to wait until Annie could get out again in the morning. In the meantime she had some thinking to do.

EIGHT

Ma was singing when Annie brought Tate back for supper. It wasn't the loud kind of raucous noise you expected from rolling drunkards in the street and taverns open far too early. This was quieter, she was singing to herself. As much as Annie wanted her mother to be happy, it was always strange to see her in a good mood. Especially because very good moods could be closely followed by very bad ones. Dinner wasn't anything special, potatoes fried in oil. The leftover oysters had been diced to make a stuffing on the side, it was more bread than oyster, but there was enough. She knew better than to try and squirrel away even an extra mouthful. There was nothing new to be found in the room, but Ma smiled more than she usually did, and Annie could only smell the booze if she stood really close. The quiet humming kept going even while Annie was staring at the ceiling waiting for sleep, the room's one window closed and barred against the thin summer moonlight. The warm pile of bodies and blankets was usually a safe haven at the end of the day.

Instead of making her feel comfortable and happy, Ma's singing simply made her feel dread.

Annie stayed awake later than anybody else in the house. It was never quiet in the rookery, there was always somebody awake at every hour, bodies moving, people shouting, yelling, talking. Night was a little more sacrosanct, punishments for disturbing your neighbors ran from a cuff to the head to a knife in the ribs. It never failed to surprise Annie just how much noise people made, and how unsettling it was when that noise was lessened by the night.

She'd slipped the square of paper into the hidden pocket in her nightgown before she went to bed. When she woke an hour or more before the sun came through the cracks around the window, she had a dull ache in her side where one of the corners pressed into her as she slept. She felt like she'd been struggling in her sleep, like fighting in a nightmare. She didn't dare say anything, she didn't even dare rub the sore spot, lest Ma figure out she had a secret.

Leftover potatoes warmed over the stove made the breakfast. There were bees in the huts on the roof and Ma did the sewing for the beekeeper so they had a spot of honey, carefully guarded and carefully doled out using the smallest of the spoons.

Ma being in a good mood meant that Tate was in a sour one. He dropped things and threw things and generally made a lot of noise. His usually cheerful demeanor was gone, like he was aware that he was not the reason that Ma was happy and he didn't seem too happy with that idea. Ma took all of his fussing with surprising good grace. Annie still took him out to play with Mrs. Kimberbokker's boy as soon as breakfast was over, then skipped out to go find Mary.

NINE

Annie flipped the folded square of paper over and over around her fingertips, the dark sigil coming and going as the light hit it. The morning light through the wooden slats was not quite enough to read by. Mary was gone, no one had seen her since the previous day's pursuit. Annie didn't know what to do, so she'd simply told anyone who asked that they hadn't got the paper yet. She'd considered going back to look for Mary, but their last conversation played over in her head. "Ne'er go back." Mary'd said. Annie wanted to believe she was right. Mary knew lots more about how things were supposed to work, she'd always been right before. But there was right and there was Right. Annie wasn't sure Mary knew about the difference.

Annie tucked the paper back into her sleeve and gathered up her skirts. She needed to find Mary, wherever she was hiding, before she handed the page over to Ida.

She wormed her way out of the wooden box, blinking a little as her eyes adjusted. None of the other kiddos were about, the ones who'd come for tasks had already headed out and Ida had long since gone back inside. The little scrap of dirt was bare of all but footprints and the usual broken halves of crates and barrel-staves. No sign of Mary. Anne hadn't heard Ida ask about her either. So it was up to her.

The best place to start looking is the last place you saw what you lost. Granted, Ma had been talking about the thimble, a shiny silver thing that couldn't move about on its own, of course, but Annie figured the same idea would work with a person. Ma's voice in her head trumped Mary's offhand advice. She had to go back to 24th Street and figure out what happened from there.

"Oi, Annie." The voice that piped up was thin, reedy. Annie didn't recognize it. She whipped around, surprised, looking for the source. A head was just visible behind the retaining wall. The little boy was half her size and probably weighed less than a bucket o' wet mice. He cast a quick glance at the back door of the dive.

"Mary sez ta meet her at the docks and bring the prybar."

"Mary sez what?"

But he had already scarpered, little puffs of dust left hanging in his wake.

At the docks? Annie knew more about the docks than most places in the neighborhood, but she'd never been there with Mary. She wasn't sure where to find her. Still the docking area was only so big and she hadn't picked up a task from Ida today. She didn't relish the idea of lugging the crowbar all the way down to the waterside, she was going to have to be a little more clever about carrying it this time.

"Grab her."

The command was all the warning Annie got. She ducked and spun without looking, pulling her arms and shoulders in tight to make a smaller target. She still got caught, the one that grabbed her was too experienced to be fooled, he grabbed for her waist and her spin carried her right into his grip. She spat and struggled, trying to find the weak point in his embrace, but he lifted her the hands breadth needed to keep her feet from finding purchase in the dirt.

Yesterday's incident still fresh in her mind, Annie exhaled, pulled up her feet and sagged, slipping through the circle of his arms and down until her butt hit the ground.

"Oh criminy, Pete. Just get a hand on her and bring her along."

Annie rolled away, just enough to spring to her feet without tripping over her skirts. The voice was Ida's. She felt in her pocket for the scraps of brick. Mary'd been right, Ida was *upta sumpin'*. Annie's quick flash to fury settled into a slower burn. She considered her options. She could fight this guy, try to scratch him up, but he was one of Dirty Mike's guys. That meant trouble for her even if she managed to escape.

Instead, Annie carefully dusted off her skirts.

"I can come along my own self." Annie was surprised to hear the defiance in her own voice.

Ida had a raised an eyebrow and smirked. "Fat Teddy wants to see ya."

Annie didn't know Fat Teddy, had only ever heard the name. Maybe going along with Ida wasn't such a good idea after all, but she was committed now. She threw her shoulders back and shook off another one of Pete's grasping hands. Three broad steps brought her nose to chin with Ida.

The older girl looked surprised but didn't back down. Annie didn't think she'd ever seen Ida back down. It made Annie scared, breathless, she felt as if just the right move would tip the balance in her favor. Her fingers tightened on the rough knot of brick in her pocket.

Ida arched an eyebrow at her.

"You want me to come with you, Ida, ya just gotta ask. You dinna need to be so flippin' bossy." Annie kept her voice even, put the energy she felt into the sound of her voice, not the loudness of it.

Ida looked her up and down with something halfway between a sneer and a smile sketched across her lips.

"Not a mouse anymore, eh Annie? Word on the street is you've turned out more of a cat." Ida made a clawing motion with her fingertips. Word of yesterday's fight against the Aelfheid boy must have trickled through the grapevine. Annie kept her mouth closed and her chin up.

"Hold yer tongue and don't make me look bad." Ida's lips decided on a smile, but the sort that soured your stomach.

"What fer?"

"Someone bashed Thomas' head in last night. You and Mary were supposed ta be working him so Teddy wants to ask ya aboot it."

Annie's soul went cold. Not at the mention of a murder, but at the mention of Mary in the same breath. It meant trouble, she was sure of it.

"From what we saw he was a bit of an ass." Annie put forth, as casually as possible. "Didja ask the cuckold?" She had to be careful now, use the words Mary would. She had to say all the right things or her newfound energy would be lost.

That got a proper smile out of Ida. *Good*, Annie thought. She didn't like the idea of being questioned with an enemy at her back, at least if she was smiling, Ida might come down on her side of things.

"Which cuckold? There was three at last count." Ida strode

on ahead, Annie just a pace behind. The two ne'er-do-wells following at an arm's length made Annie smile in spite of herself. Ida had come expecting a fight. It meant she was taking Annie a little more seriously.

"Busy man," Annie responded, not because she had an opinion, but because she'd heard Ma use the same response.

"Not anymore." Ida smirked.

Their path took them out of the alley and back up the street, through the front doors of the Tavern. Ida was showcasing, Annie realized. She wanted the rest of the Gophers to see her bringing Annie in for an accounting. Annie kept her head up, shoulders thrown back. Damned if she was going to slink in like a dog that'd been caught in the cupboard. Early morning though, the Tavern was half-empty, only the all-nighters huddled in the corners, sleeping off the night before. Annie breathed a sigh of relief.

Fat Teddy weighed maybe a hunnert pounds soaking wet. Tall enough to brush the ceilings if he stood on tiptoe, pale watery eyes that looked like green frogs eggs and a sixth finger on each hand meant he weren't a local, he'd come to High Charity from someplace Annie would probably never see. He held court in the back room of the tavern, thick stone walls and thick wooden doors kept the noise out and the secrets in.

"This the one?" he asked Ida. Annie stood just to her right, chin up, still unrestrained. A quick scan of the room showed Dirty Mike in the corner, making notes in a tiny book with a tiny stylus. He glanced up when the doors opened, then turned back to his notes, not acknowledging either girl standing there.

"Aye." Ida replied. "Gave the job ta Mary 'n Annie. Bettin' Mary nicked yer paper and done-in Thomas ta cover it up." Annie recognized what the older girl was doing. Setting up the story, laying groundwork so when questions came up they'd already have an easy answer.

Teddy shut the door behind them and crossed the room in a single stride. Annie had never seen legs quite that long. He folded himself up and tucked in behind the long table at the back of the room. Annie couldn't take her eyes off him. There was a humming in her head, the lamps burned a shade more blue.

"There's more spellstuff in the room," Teddy reported disinterestedly. "The lasses brought it in with them."

Mike nodded.

Ida put her hands to her waist, rubbing a carved wooden toggle on her belt between thumb and forefinger. Annie recognized it, a counter-charm against evil, used to belong to Ginger, but somehow Ida'd scammed him out of it.

The corner of Annie's sleeve felt heavy, like she'd accidentally stashed a brickbat there.

"All right Annie, tell us what you know." Mike tipped his chair back forward onto all four legs with a thunk.

Annie's tongue clove to the roof of her mouth. There was something unnatural going on. Something she couldn't quite get her head around. The words made an effort to bubble up, unbidden, only to be stopped before they reach her lips.

Spellstuff, she realized. Teddy had some kind of magic going on that could make her tell things. She'd heard rumors about Teddy bein' some kinda wizard, but she'd always thought they were just rumors to cover up something worse.

She cast a wide-eyed glance to Teddy, eyes closed and sitting at all angles in the back, then to Mike who had suddenly become much more interested in the proceedings.

"Gwaaan." Ida gave Annie a shove, pushing the smaller girl

forward a step. With an abrupt pop Annie's tongue was free of whatever spellstuff Teddy had going on. She worked it around in her mouth, wetting her lips before she spoke. Now the words were hers, whatever Teddy had been up to had been pushed out of her head.

"Mary and I, we showed up out back the tavern, like we always do, to figure out what to do with the day," Annie started slowly.

You gotta know who you're talking to. Ma's voice whispered in her head, unbidden. *Don't use big words on simple folks, don't swear in front of anybody with shoes better than yours.* Annie paused and chose her next words a little differently, a little less "Starchie" as Mary would say.

"Ida here tol' us Mike needed sumpin' lifted and he was payin' a marker fer it." She caught Mike's eye as she spoke. He nodded. So far so good.

"So did Mary nick the paper and Thomas catch her at it? Or was she just impatient?" Ida interrupted, continuing to push her version of what happened, even though she wasn't even there. Annie felt a silver flash of irritation from Ma, as well, the version of Ma in her head anyway.

"Ida, you weren't there so shut yer yap." Annie spoke sharply, though she was sure she'd pay for it later. "We spent that whole day following Thomas. Guy must've shaken every hand on Market Street, scammed an orange off one of the girls. Mary said it was all the kind of stuff she expected he'd be doin'. Took forever, but Mary ain't ever in a hurry. She gets the job done right the first time."

"So she never got the paper?" Mike asked pointedly.

"Oh, we got it. Mary snuck in through the back door of the defender's office and lifted the wallet out of his coat." Annie fished about in her sleeve and retrieve the folded packet. It stung her fingers, like she was trying to keep a grip on a fog of biting gnats. She couldn't wait to be rid of it. She held it a second longer despite the stings, just to be sure it was her decision, before passing it to Ida with a flourish.

Mike burst out laughing. Ida looked furious, eyebrows was drawn down, a pair of elevens appearing in the wrinkles between her eyes. Ida began to unfold the paper.

"Wait." Mike held up a hand.

Ida rolled her eyes in a supremely cheeky expression of disdain. "I've gots a counter charm." She tapped the carved wooden toggle, then returned her attention to the packet.

Teddy opened one eye, looked her up and down, but before he could open his mouth she popped the square open and scanned the contents.

Annie wasn't sure why she bothered, everyone knew Ida couldn't read three letters past her own name.

Annie felt briefly ill, like the whole room had suddenly been filled with smoke and ash. In the corner of her vision, the walls of the room seemed to flex, then it, whatever it was, passed. The hum in her head was gone, the lights returned to their normal warm yellow. Teddy shrugged and closed his eyes again.

Ida passed the paper to Mike, the vertical lines between her eyebrows, right where Ma usually placed her moon-mark, standing out like streaks of charcoal before they faded away. Annie frowned. That weren't right. She knew a wrinkle when she saw one, but what had started as an expression of displeasure on Ida's face had turned into…something else. Mike didn't seem to notice anything amiss. He took the paper gingerly and passed it to Teddy. Teddy waved it off. "Safe enough now," he mumbled and fished a long thin pipe out of his coat. Mike cocked an eyebrow at him, disbelieving for a moment before turning his attention back to Annie.

"Well, Ida, it looks like I owe someone a marker." Mike tucked the square of paper away in his waistcoat. "But it still don't let Mary off the hook."

"Why would Mary knock off Thomas? The job's done, and Mary hates a mess," Annie pointed out. She'd recovered her wits quick enough once Teddy's spellstuff had worn off, and she wasn't about to let Ida roll Mary under the cart. The fire in her belly was back and Annie held onto it, using it to fuel her defense of her friend.

"Thomas was still livin' when Mary and I scarpered, we met back up at the Promenade after we made sure no one what followed us. Mary weren't covered in blood or actin' weird or nothin'."

"She could've kilt him after ya split." Ida countered.

"Enough." Mike stepped in just as Annie balled up her fists to take a swing at the larger girl.

"He was kilt with a prybar, Annie." Ida practically snarled. "Face bashed in and left lyin' in the alleyway. Everybody knows Mary carries that damn thing around with her all the time."

"I know she does, we used it ta get the door open, ya cow. Mary had me hide it for safekeeping, I know where it's at and Mary ain't got it, so shut your yellin'." Annie turned, fed up with Ida and her trouble making. "Mary *ain't kilt* nobody, so stop saying it. Just sayin' it over and over it don't turn it inta a true thing." Annie repeated angrily. This was not a fight she could win, Ida was older, had a reputation, had the ear of more than just one or two of the lads, but something in Annie couldn't let it go.

"I said enough." Mike stepped in. Annie was grateful, no real good could come out of her socking Ida in the face.

"Annie, bring in Mary's crowbar so we kin cross her off the King's Guard's list."

"The King's Guard? You sent ta Guard after her?" Annie was outraged. All the gangs turned members over to the Guard. Usually the disloyal, the ones who murdered out of turn, troublemakers all. The Black Hall was a useful deterrent and helped keep the peace, as long as certain palms were greased and coffers kept full.

"T'was me that done it." Ida retorted. "Spitters ain't going to put up with us killin' Thomas, but if Mary goes to the Black Hall that's good enough. This way we don't have to take it to the streets."

"Ida, I think you done plenty." Mike pointed to the door. "If Mary's in the clear, she's in the clear, we don't sacrifice our own for something this small. We gotta find the one with blood on his hands.

TEN

"Yer daft. Guys like Mike don't use spellstuff, they don't gotta." Mary dangled her legs over the edge of the dock, the prybar in question on the worn wood between them. "Their business is all arrangements and grift." The air stank of fish and pitch but otherwise being down by the edge of the river was a welcome relief from the closed-in heat of the city. The docks were fair game, like the Promenade, they were under the thumb of the King's Guard so the ever-present turf war between the Spitters and the Gophers was kept streets away.

"I'm tellin' ya, Teddy's got some kind of spellstuff going on, sumpin' that makes you tell things you don't wanna tell." Annie drummed her heels against the wooden slats. "It was weird and it was creepy."

She and Mary planned to head back to the Hopper together, prybar in tow, to clear Mary's name with Mike. No one had seen Ida, which was probably for the best. Annie might have thought about throwing a punch, but Mary might have hit her with the prybar just out of spite.

"Teddy ain't local, he's one o' them from the far south, yanno, that island with the hunnert foot tall trees? They're called Aelfheid er summat. With the vowels all slidey." Mary made a big show of twisting her whole face around as she repeated the name. "Aaaeeeeuuuulfheyyyyd. Mike jes' calls 'em Clingers."

"He's got an extra stubby finger on each hand, sticks out ta other side, like a thumb. Aelfheid got too many toes, this guy weren't one o' them." Annie confided, glancing around to be sure they weren't overheard. Ma's silvery voice in her head reminded her not to gossip.

"Prolly 'cos o all the trees where he's from. Bet he's a heck of a climber," Mary mused.

"Can't climb in High Charity much. Maybe the sides o' buildings, but that'd be weird," Annie said.

"Tellin' tales agin, Mary?"

Both girls shared a horrified look, then turned as one to see Ida behind them, Ginger at her back. The sun was behind her, making her halo of golden hair glow.

"Me?" Mary flushed red. "You done told errybody I kilt Thomas, ya fat cow!"

Ida didn't dignify the truth with a response. She stepped up and, with a booted foot, kicked the prybar off the dock and into the water.

"IDA!" Annie scrambled to her feet just a half-second slower than Mary, who'd lunged at the older girl and missed by a hair.

"'Cos it's the truth," Ida declared. "Ya mighta done the job Mike set ya, but now we gotta dustup with the Spitter's comin' and it's all on you."

"Ain't the truth, Ida," Annie said firmly, stepping up and taking a stance between the two rivals. "I dunno what yer upta, but Mary ain't kilt anyone."

"Well, now we just have her word for it, don't we." Ida sneered.

"Imma kill you next…" Mary made a lunge for Ida, but Annie stood in the way, keeping the girls apart.

"Take it up with Mike," Ida called over her shoulder. "Assumin' the King's Guard don't get ta ya first."

"King's Guard? Annie, Mike handed me over ta the King's Guard?" Mary turned on her friend now, shock and disbelief written across her face.

"We can get it fixed." Annie caught her arm. We just need ta get Mike the prybar so he can see it ain't the one that kilt…" Her words stuttered and slowed as the events of the past few moments came together to paint a picture.

"We ain't got the prybar." Mary said grimly. "Ida took care o' that."

Annie and Mary stared down into the inky water.

"I'm gonna kill her. If I'm on the hook for Thomas, I'm sending Ida ta join him."

ELEVEN

Annie blinked back a tear. Crying here and now would get her into more trouble than anything else. Her arm ached from where it was twisted up behind her back. It was Ginger that had her pinned, Ida's boy. Mary and Ida faced each other down across the muddy patch of yard like a pair of angels after the fall. Ida just sneered, she was half a head taller than Mary and held a fish knife down close to her side. Mary held a smaller blade close to her chest, neither girl giving anything away. Ginger was distracted. They all were. Women fought dirty, women fought alone. A brawl between two men could easily set the whole room to fisticuffs. When the ladies got serious, no one wanted to get caught in the crossfire. Annie closed her eyes and shifted her weight so she was balanced on both feet. Her left arm was free, her own knife just in reach, but sticking a blade into Ginger was dangerous. It was a step too far and might get her more than a fist to the face.

She waited as his grip slackened, the flurry of skirts and curses pulling his attention. Annie rolled, twisting her free shoulder into his chest and giving the taller boy a sharp shove.

It worked. He let go to grab for support and Annie pulled her arm free. She dropped and scrambled forward toward where Mike and his cronies were holding court. She dodged Ginger's groping arm, steering him into one of the other men with another quick shove. He was already off-balance and he keeled over, long legs tangling up and taking another man with him. Annie slipped up beside Mike to watch her two friends as they broke apart again. This time right blood staining the sleeve of Ida's shirt. The taller girl spat curses at Mary, fishing knife held straight out like an accusatory finger.

"Got sumpin' ta say, Annie?" Mike didn't look at her, but the words seemed to fall in her direction.

"Can you make 'em stop?" Around the two of them, the ruckus seemed to die down, like they were encased in a glass bubble. Annie felt a humming in her head, her heart, like Fat Teddy's spellstuff but somehow crisper, cleaner. She felt inspired.

""Aye. But I know better than to get in the middle of a catfight."

"They're fighting over a lie, Mike, that ain't right."

Mike snorted. "Ain't about right. It's about who's boss. Can't have a ship with two captains." He raised an eyebrow and glanced in her direction. "Which one are you gonna follow when all this is done. The one who stays or the one who goes?"

"Ain't going to matter if one of them is dead."

"Good point." He shrugged.

The two girls circled one another in the open space. Annie knew who the winner would be. Ida had friends among the adults, she was practically a grownup herself. Mary might be more popular with the kiddos, but not a one of the little ones could stand up to Ida's influence.

"Mike, my marker. I'm calling it in." Annie's words spilled out and hung in the air between them. On the other side of the courtyard, the tip of the moon had peeked over the rooftops, the glow still too thin to show against the lamplight.

"You're going to spend it now? On that sorry lot?" That got his full attention. The light caught the scar that ran from cheek to lip, throwing it into sharp relief, like Tok himself had marked him with a fingernail.

"Yes." Annie answered clearly and softly. Making a scene would end badly, it felt like the entire crowd was full of malice, ready to blow if even one word or gesture was paid out wrong. She took a calming breath, then another. The space around them brightened, the moonlight streaming over the top of Hoppers, cutting through the rising dust and filling in the shadows cast by the lamps. Ma was going to give her holy whatfor for staying out after the lamps were lit, but in this moment, it didn't matter.

"You're an odd one, I'll give you that Annie." Mike shook his head. The world felt disconnected. Annie's quiet conversation with Dirty Mike framed against the roiling crowd and snarling women. Mary and Ida had closed again, this time Ida got her fists into Mary's hair. She held her rival to the ground and pinned her face down, one knee in her back.

Annie held her breath.

Mike spot and held up his hands. "Enough."

Ida didn't listen, hauling Mary's head back to expose the white of her throat. She meant to kill her, of that Annie was sure. Ida's eyes were wild, her teeth bared in a lioness grin. On her forehead, twin lines like the number eleven were sketched in shadow. The symbol for Tok. Annie knew in a flash just what had played out. Whatever had passed on to Ida from the cursed paper must have control of her now. Annie felt cold. Annie felt angry. Mixed in there, deep in the back of her mind, she felt ashamed she hadn't understood sooner.

"Enough." Mike's voice rang out, this time at full volume, bouncing off the courtyard walls and rattling the eardrums of everyone present. Ida's arm didn't stop. She brought the keen edge of the knife up against Mary's throat in a move used to slit the throats of sheep and rabbits.

Mike didn't try to block it, he simply took a step forward and delivered a kick that snapped Ida's hand to the side and flung her to the ground.

Ida shook her head and reached for the knife that had clattered to the dirt.

"I said enough, Ida. I ain't having blood on my hands tonight. Ya won, be happy with that."

Annie recognized the sour, surly look. Ida was drunk, not on liquor, but on the power of life and death. Annie had seen that look before on men who had been given one too many kicks to the head. Ma got the same look when she'd been drinking. Acolytes got the same look when the church pews were full and the collection dishes brimming. Tok wasn't in control, Annie realized with a shock. Ida wasn't a puppet. She was a willing participant.

Ida made the blade disappear into her skirts and got to her feet. The black double bars on her forehead fading. No one else seemed to see them, to remark on them. Mike didn't move to help her up, neither did anyone else.

"You." Mike pointed at Mary. "Get out, you're done here." Mary spat dirt and blood and struggled to get to her feet, skirts trapped under her knees. Annie ran over to give her a hand up, but the older girl shook her head. She got to her feet her ownself and stared defiantly at Ida, eyes bright blue amid a bruised and muddy face.

Slowly, like a feral cat backing away from a terrier, Mary turned and made her way out to the alley behind the courtyard. Three Toed Tom and Kelly followed, Tom pausing just long enough to spit in the dirt at Ida's feet. Confusion flashed across Ida's face, swiftly replaced by the slow burn of anger.

Mike chuckled. "Just because you won don't mean everyone's gonna like it. Let 'em go." he waved at Tess and the older woman came over, taking Ida's arm.

"Take the winner inside and get her a drink." Mike instructed. Tess' grin would have been unpleasant even without the gaps in her teeth.

"Annie." Mike turned back to where Annie was trying to shrink back into the crowd. Mike flapped a hand at the remaining kids clustered around the far end of the alley. "Keep the kids in the line, I'll have Donner hand out jobs in the mornin'."

Annie felt as if all the blood had drained out into her shoes. She felt like she managed to lose both of her friends in a single swoop. Mary was gone. Ida was…Promoted? She cast a glance at Ida, now the center of a knot of men and women all cheering and laughing as they jockeyed their way back into the bar. Ida was grinning, though a bit uncertainly. She didn't look back, not even once.

"Oi, Annie. This means you're the boss now, don't it?" Jimmy had appeared to her left, Rico and Shy Malia behind him, the kiddos creeping in from the fringes where they'd been watching.

"Donner's boss, Annie's just boss until he gets here at sunup," Shy Malia chimed in. She dismissed both Mary and Ida with a flip of her braids.

With the adults all back inside, just the kids of varying sizes were left out in the courtyard, gathered into clumps and clusters.

Nearly half a dozen had followed Mary when she left. Annie's mind raced as one by one the remaining kids met her eyes, some with defiance, some uncertain for a second before they glanced away. She could step up, become one of them that gets noticed and risks a bit for a Reputation, or she could follow Mary out and leave the kids to whoever stepped up next.

Except, abandoning all her friends wasn't really a question.

"All right, you lot!" Annie waved of them all over. "Come here and listen up." She mounted the steps at the back of the tavern. "First up. Ida's out. She wants to join the grownups, fine. But she ain't the boss of nunna you anymore. Anything the Gophers want ye to do goes through Donner or me now, just like it used to go through Ida. She's a grown-up now, she gets ta hang inside, so she can't be trusted anymore, got it?"

They all nodded, the youngest ones looking to the oldest ones before agreeing.

"What…What about Mary?" Rico was the smallest kid there, hair so pale it matched his fair skin. His voice was as soft as a ghost's sigh, but when he chose to speak, everyone listened.

"Mary's out. I don't like it." Annie held up a hand to stall their protest. "If I can get her back in, I will, but you saw who went with her. She might not come back, and she might make her own place, so in the meantime give her and the others a bit a-road. Don't let them mess with our stuff, but don't go after them neither, not until we figger out what Mary's gonna do."

Annie took a mental note of who was left. Five of the kids were handy in a fight. She had more girls than boys, which meant they were going to need to be smart, not tough. Ma said leadership changes, whether it be kings, gang leaders or the big bully in a group of little kids, meant that all their enemies were going to start showing up.

"If any of you want to go with Mary, now's the time. Otherwise I'm boss tonight."

No one moved. Shy Malia punched her in the shoulder. "Are you kidding? Now we might actually get to *be* summat instead of just waitin' on the grownups."

Annie took a breath. "Alright, back to your homes and hidey holes. We'll meet up here in the morning just like we always do. Go in twos and threes if you can, anyone who's got a grudge is going to come gunning for us until we show our stuff."

They all knew the drill, they'd all seen regime changes before. They all nodded, almost as one, then shot into the alley like dry beans hitting the floor.

Annie was alone, she realized. She and Mary had always teamed up, watching each other's backs. The kids had scattered into their usual pairs of twos and threes, but without Mary, Annie was looking at a long walk in the moonlit dark. Ma was going to horsewhip her for coming through the warded door after sundown. She cast a glance over her shoulder to the warmth of the gaslamp that hung outside the tavern door, then back at the black and empty alley

"Ownself, then." Annie whispered and set off into the dark, the blessed Moonlight painting the path ahead.

Wishes Folded Into Fancy Paper

Kimberly Unger

ONE

Della folded and unfolded the stiff paper against her naked thigh until its surface was covered by a fine pattern of creases. With a twist of her fingers, she popped the folded token into its final shape, mimicking the bold and waxy flowers of the Likki tree, native to Nami and Papap's home planet. This was one of the specials, a pattern used only for Family members. Fancy paper token folding, the substitution of cleverly folded tokens for chains of over-harvested blooms, had been cribbed from the Imported traditions and turned, ultimately, into an opportunity. Nami and Pappap had carved out their own space, imported more family members from off planet, and established themselves as premier Fancy-makers through shrewd business and finger-numbing labor that passed from children to grandchildren.

Della finished with the token and dropped it into the basket beside her. The midyear sun was hot, the smell of the linen shirt she wore to protect against sunburn mixing with sweat and salt. No sunscreen allowed, that smell was too strong for the Gira's sensitive noses and the Riuu valued salt as a resource, they said it smelled of wealth. So Della labored on in the 5th season heat, adding her inadvertent essence to the folded paper flowers.

"UUUUUUUuuuuuUUUuuuuuuugh." Mix drew the vowels out as long as possible, the ups and downs forming a rough melody before she dropped the consonants in. The stringing for family patterns was slow and far more complex than what they created for sale. Della was only halfway done with the folds, so Mix would have to take her time.

"What's gotten into you?" Della failed to keep the irritation out of her voice. Mix was agitated, unraveling yet another mistake in the knotting. The frustrated action devolving into futile yanking, making the knots tighter rather than unraveling them. The handful of folded tokens on the younger sibling's lap drifted to the rug, stirring the dust. Mix picked them up in a bunch, dropping them back into the basket to start over. Della tutted and reached in to make sure none of them had crumpled. She'd have to steam out any wrinkles if they had and that might affect the value of the whole Fancy.

"Just issues." The flat, short sentence meant they were the kind of issues that Nami or the other grandparents would pick apart and analyze, lay bare the flaws. It was deeply uncomfortable relationship stuff the way only the elders had real reference for.

Della carried on, playing deliberately obtuse. "Issues? You mean like relationship issues? I haven't seen Lena come to pick you up for a few days, you two OK?" Of course she knew they weren't. Della pretended not to notice, stayed out of the way and waited for Mix to give her an opening. Her younger sister had been distracted for weeks, despondent when she thought nobody was looking. She'd been arriving at the shop early and leaving late, staying around for dinner and cigars instead of skipping out to meet Lena the moment the dishes had been cleared.

"Well."

Della waited through a pause three knots long while Mix finished untangling the strings. "Lena is matriculating," she said sourly.

"I heard. That's pretty huge." Della chose her words carefully, neutrally. Mix and Lena as a couple was not popular conversation in the household. Some of the family had come around, some were still convinced it was all just a phase. It had closed some doors, caused a few fights. It was more internal turmoil than the family had seen in a decade. Nami was delighted, she loved a good disruption. Della was tired and stayed out of it all as much as possible, except to offer her support to Mix when she got the chance.

"Yes, but." Mix hesitated again. "It means a big change. Lena's going to be out of the household and s/he wants me to go too. You know the Gira kick their kids out after matriculation, disown them for the next five years. It's not fair, how can s/he succeed without support, without a family?"

"Ah." Della folded two tokens and dropped them in the basket during the pause that followed. The Gira families were larger, children were an investment that could number in the tens and twenties, the Riuu spawned thousands with survival numbering in the ones and twos. Both cultures were a little hard for her to wrap her head around. "Do you want to go with her?"

"Well, I guess yes... And no. Which sounds stupid, I know, but it seems so haphazard. The Gira chuck a bunch of tokens at the kids and lock them out of their homes. How messed up is that?"

"It is a *lot* of tokens, more than Nami and Papap had in their pockets when they came here. And they don't have to kill a lion with a stick, or spend the next eight days getting pricked with urchin spines all over their body, or learn a dance that lasts three days, or any of the other things people have done to become adults. They just have to stand on their own two feet." Della felt uncomfortable defending the Gira to Mix, of all people.

Mix gave her a look, the "you're not my mother" look.

"Yeah, yeah, I get it," she said. "But usually a class tends to group up, you know? Band together, get themselves new digs, new gigs. Lena doesn't… No one wants to team up because s/he's been hanging out with me. I think I screwed up h/her life."

Mix carefully started again, nimble fingertips forming the knots that would space the tokens apart and give the Fancy its structure.

"Sounds complicated." Della was careful to stay neutral, to give Mix the space to speak.

"Yeah, I mean, I love Lena, I want to spend the rest of my life with Lena, but I feel like there's no plan, like there never was a plan, just love. Love really sucks at planning, have you ever noticed that?"

"Love sucks at planning." Della agreed. "I'm stealing that for a new token fold. But it is never too late you know, for the planning part."

"Well, yeah. I'm just not sure if Lena is ready for me to do any planning."

"The two of you have been an item for years now. Are you ready for a change?" Della rifled through the pile of tokens, looking for a particular faded blue. Token ink tended to be impermanent, it faded over time, giving her a range of pastels on top of the fresh, new primary colors. It gave her a chance to tell stories with the subtlety she never managed to pull off in real life.

"No. I like how we are now. I don't want to change, but I'm going to have to if we're going to stay together."

"You *both* have to, it's not just one way. Well, it's not supposed to be." Subtlety was best saved for the token-folding, Della reflected. "Remember your first date with Lena?"

"Oh yeah, it was awful."

"Was every date exactly the same?"

"No. Most better, some worse."

"The rest of your lives are not going to be any different. You are going to have good days, you're going to have bad days. Things will suck and things will be amazing. Is Lena the person who can put up with your shit when the bad days happen?"

"I suppose."

"Suppose?" Mix grimaced and returned to the braiding, scooping tokens from the bucket one at a time to add them to the Fancy. Della gave her a moment to settle before shouldering on.

"Look, Mix." She said. "It doesn't matter in the end what I think, or what Nami and Papap or Lena's family think. What matters is what you and Lena want. You two need to be together on this, all in, win or lose, or you need to each go back to your own comfort zones."

"But what if we lose?"

"Mix, you *know* how many times Nami and Papap lost before our family came to this planet. You're going to lose sometimes, we're all going to lose. That's a given. Do you get up again is the question. Do you think Lena can get up again with you?" Della asked.

Mix was very quiet for a minute, the whisk-whisk sound of the silken twine filling the space.

"The Gira only get one shot. They're not like us. Win or Lose. If Lena doesn't succeed, s/he's done," she said mournfully.

"What the hell, Mix?"

Her sib's startled look from between black eyebrows betrayed an inner cowardice.

"Are you really going to buy into that? You're both already pissing everyone the hell off just by being together. Why let any of that stop you now?"

It was back, that quick, easy grin that lit up her sister from the inside. "It's not really that simple, but maybe we can get up and try again."

"Damn right you can. Now get back to work. Nami says we can go get candy-fluff if we finish before lunch."

"Really? You fell for that?"

TWO

Papap had first shown Della what to do back when she was young enough to believe in things like curses and hopefuls. Young enough where intent could fade between one recess and another and one morning's enemy could be one afternoon's best friend.

The Fancy for sale in the shop, the ones they made to just pick up and go, were nearly unreadable. Action, glory, legacy, anticipation, all mashed up, barely in order. Assembled to be pretty, to suit the design sense of the Indigenous, not sensible and story-centric like the Imported. Once in a while, seated on the tall stool behind the register, six-year old Della could see coherence, most often in Nami's sale Fancy. For family friends, for the rare customers who understood the context of the Fancy, exceptions were made. Those exceptions came with an unspoken price and could almost never be bought, only bestowed.

"A unique Fancy is a great gift. Did Mix ask you to fold it for them?" Papap moved to stir the fire in the fireplace. All three summers were warm and dry, but the solitary winter was cold and wet, the rain freezing in sheets over the windows, covering the walkways, sometimes sealing them in the house for days at a time. Those were Della's favorite days because she could stay in the back room of the shop by the fire and ask all the questions that came into her head.

A frown creased Della's eyebrows. "You know better, Papap. It's bad-luck for Family to ask for something new, it has to come from the soul of the giver."

Papap pursed his lips together, considering. "Treat it carefully then, the Gira do not follow the same path as we do. Lena's family may not respect what you have done."

"I know, Papap, let me show you."

Della retrieved a fresh token and held it against her thigh. The rough edges of the practice paper plucked at the fine threads of her tights. Quickly, eagerly, she made the creases, back and forth and…

She stared at the results, a compilation of bad angles and sharp points with little symmetry. The points pricked her fingers, the edges caught on her skin. She was sure she didn't make a mistake, sure she had followed the motions that she had been practicing, but the twisted thing she held her hand held none of the beauty she remembered.

"Ah. So." Papap lifted the angry construction with his fingertips and flicked it into the fireplace.

"I'm sorry, I must've missed a fold, Papap."

"Sometimes the folds reflect what is inside, Della. You are upset."

"I am…frustrated." Della stared into the fire, watching the flames chomp away at the folded edges first.

Papap grimaced, a resigned gesture. "I know you and I have been at odds about Mix and Lena."

"I just don't…I don't understand why you don't want Mix to be happy."

Papap was quiet for a long moment, seeing something different in the dance of the flames. "I want Mix to be happy. I am not sure that Lena's family has the same hope," he said finally. "But perhaps it is time to say something nice and see what they say in return."

"OK, Papap, let's say something nice. We can send them a proper curse later if we have to." Della grinned at the idea. Tradition held that curses, proper curses folded into Fancy, needed an iron will to make them come to pass. Papap had taught her the technique, but it had always seemed like far too much work to Della.

She began again with a fresh set of practice tokens, folding back and forth until, with a twist and a flourish, the flower emerged. Something unlike anything she'd ever seen in a shop. With a crow of victory, she passed it into Papap's trembling fingers.

"Well, it's certainly not traditional." Papap said, turning the Fancy over in his hands. "You've got both kinds of folds in here, Indigenous and Import." He held it up to the light, tracing a finger along the staggered curve that formed the heart of the pattern. "And there's more than one token in here."

"I used three, one for Mix, one for Lena, one for something different." Della gestured to the pile of discarded practice tokens. "It's a matriculation present, do you think Lena will like it?"

"And you designed this as a standalone, a Posey? It won't fit into a Fancy, why not?"

Della folded her hands in her lap. She knew Papap would understand if she came at it from just the right direction. "Papap, you are not the only one who doesn't agree with Mix and Lena being together."

Papap frowned. "I see."

"I can modify this pattern for use later in a Fancy, as Mix and Lena's own family grows and their story gets told. It seemed better to have it start out as a standalone, the very first fold of a whole new history."

He turned it over in his fingertips, carefully testing the sharpness of the folds, the flex of the leaves. "Love is unplanned. That's what it says?"

"It was something Mix said. 'Love sucks at planning'. They both just sort of jumped into their lives together and made plans as they went. Lena's matriculation is the next step in that."

Papap smiled, his eyes almost invisible amongst the creases. "I like Mix's phrase better." He carefully pulled loose one fold, then a second, then flipped and crossed the creases to reflect the missing words. "There. Love sucks at planning." He handed the folded tokens back to Della. "You're going to need a box for that, and don't forget that for good luck the tissue paper has to be blue. Lena's family will be insulted otherwise."

THREE

The funeral lasted less than 30 minutes. Nami had got the call the night before, a hysterical, incoherent Mix had not even been permitted to see the body as Lena's family swooped in and closed out h/her chapter. A "dead-line" they said, waving off Nami's condolences. Della had heard the term more than once among the Gira and Riuu who came to the shop. She just hadn't expected to see it, feel it quite so closely. Lena's suicide would be reported only at the end of the obituaries with the rest of those who had failed to rise.

"This is what happens, you see." Nami spoke quietly as the passed in the hall outside Mix's door. Della could hear the sobs from her old room where she used to bring Lena to study and discuss their future. Lena had to duck h/her head to fit through the Import-sized doorframe.

"We are too different from each other, human and the Gira."

"We get to choose, Nami." Della said firmly. "That's what makes us different from the tiger or the bird. Differences can be overcome." The old adage didn't make her feel any better, but she clung to it in the face of her guilt, of her defense of Mix and Lena.

Nami took Della's hand and patted it absently. "Sometimes, as much as we might want to, we cannot escape who we were raised to be." Nami stared at the closed door, beaten up from years of teenage tantrums and over-enthusiastic closures. "But I wish it had been so, for Lena's sake and for Mix."

"So what do we do now?"

"S/he was a part of our family. We say goodbye to Lena properly so that Mix can stand up to try again."

"Do we invite h/her family?"

"Don't be stupid, of course we invite h/her family."

"What if they don't…"

"That is not the point. They follow their tradition, we follow ours. Both traditions are worthy of these two children."

"We should say something nice back, and see how they reply." Della murmured, mind casting back to the childhood curse.

"And then we shall stand up to try again." Nami confirmed.

FOUR

"It's very simple." The Riuu pointed out. "Lena owed a debt."

Della had agreed to meet with the gangly purple insect because he'd invoked Mix's name. Like all of the Riuu, the spiky carapace, extra limbs and pincers made for a formidable appearance. Their nature, however, leaned towards balance and mediation. They were often employed as go-betweens and investigators when pride got in the way.

Mix had been hard to find since Lena's funeral nearly three months past. Now, a gangly, six-limbed Riuu and its much smaller, bluer twin stood between the two sisters. Della's sib was sulking in the back of the room, collapsed into an oversize chair, black hair tousled and unwashed.

"Lena was Gira. All debts are dissolved upon death." Della said. Try as she might to get her attention, Mix would not make eye contact. The younger woman sat, arms folded across her chest, looking quite deliberately at the floor.

"So it is, but your little sister is a human Import. Lena's debt transfers to the surviving partner according to the laws of your people."

"They weren't legally married. Lena had only just matriculated."

"A life partnership is legal upon matriculation."

"For the Gira, not for humans. You're mashing up law from both sides. You're going to have to pick one."

"There are two sides to any partnership."

Della opened her mouth to speak, but the Riuu raised a claw to stop her. "But you are right, there is no precedent, and setting one would be very expensive for everyone concerned."

"You're holding my sister hostage over Lena's debt?"

"I've been asked to acquire something unique, something new, for a client. This client has agreed to assume all of Lena's debt if you and I can come to an agreement."

"What is it you want?"

"Exclusivity." The claws snapped a command, sharp like a breaking twig. The smaller Riuu came forward with a plain fiberboard box. In the background, Mix came to attention, eyes suspicious, rimmed red with lack of sleep but bright and clear as if she'd finally found what she'd been looking for.

The lid flipped open to reveal the staggered edges and bright colors of Lena's matriculation Fancy. Mix made a sound, half outrage, half tears and lunged from the chair, arms outstretched as she tried to shoulder past the larger Riuu to get to the box.

"THAT'S OURS. YOU HAVE NO RIGHT." The Riuu sidestepped, clearly expecting Mix to make a move. The younger woman tripped and came up short, hitting the end of the tether that kept her from leaving. Della's intake of breath must have been audible because the larger Riuu clattered its mandibles sympathetically.

"Please do not be alarmed. Your sister is a credit to the warrior spirit of the Imported. We have only restrained her so we may conduct this transaction in peace." It rolled a shoulder joint ruefully. "She keeps hitting us with things."

"Give it BACK or I will do MUCH MORE than just hit you with a STICK." Mix shouted.

"As I said before, I will return it to you when our business is concluded." The Riuu turned its attention back to Della. "This pattern, this fold you have created is unique, for now. My client has agreed to buy out Lena's debt in return for instructions and exclusive use of the pattern."

Della set her arms akimbo, defiant and angry. "That's the stupidest thing I have heard today. I have no control over who copies a pattern, once it's out in public, I can't possibly keep that guarantee."

The Riuu bowed, pincers open in apology. "Forgive me, but this is what you call a "Family" pattern. That is a boundary the rest of the Imported Fancy makers will honor, and you and I both know that, without instruction, the Gira and Riuu Fancy makers will have a very hard time making a copy."

"That's not a guarantee, that's just circumstance."

"Della, don't." Mix interrupted, pleading now. Now she tried to make eye contact, now she tried to connect. Now that the situation was clear, it was Della's turn to stay incommunicado. She shook her head ever so slightly, a gesture that the agitated Mix failed to see.

The Riuu listened, Della could very faintly hear a voice in a speaker, too shrill for her to make out the words. The Client, whomever it was, was giving directions to the Riuu, which meant there was a camera nearby, that they were being observed from afar.

"It is close enough." It returned. "If you agree that you will officially bestow the pattern to my client, this will satisfy the requirement."

"And I show the folds to you?"

"No." The Riuu gestured and a camera drone dropped from the ceiling. "I'm going to record you."

Della eyeballed the hovering camera. They were common enough. This one was an indoors-only model, no call-sign, no identifiers. Papap paid the younger kids to knock any drones that came around the family compound out of the sky just in case someone was trying to copy their patterns. Ironic that one would be used to "gift" her pattern to another Fancy-maker. Bestowing a pattern was supposed to be an intimate act, bringing families closer together as they taught one another the folds. This was extortion. This was robbery.

Della made eye contact with Mix. There really was no decision to be made here. The unintended consequences, the swarm of those who saw the doomed lovers cross-cultural connection as something to be exploited had come trickling to their door like the frothy water leading a flood. Someone was taking advantage of Lena's suicide, of Mix's misery. The anger had been slow to come, overridden by her worry about her sister. Now the callousness, the sheer baseness galled Della, began to burn in her chest.

"Can I ask the name of your employer?"

The Riuu was a go-between, she reminded herself sternly. It was there to negotiate, to set the terms and persuade her if it could. There was no point wasting her ire on it.

The Riuu considered carefully before shaking its head.

"No, I don't think so. You'll know soon enough, I think, and I don't want to taint the transaction."

"Fine." Della held out a hand. "Let's see the contract".

"Della, don't," Mix pleaded. "I'll never forgive you."

FIVE

Della worked quickly, folding the creases to follow the anger in her head. Words that never reached her lips emerged in the pattern of the token, the creases and powerful detail. The Riuu's drone hung just over her shoulder, recording each and every motion of her fingers. Della allowed frustration and anger to leak out, to guide the modifications to her pattern as it flowed.

"Della, don't, please." Mix repeated the plea for the fourth or fifth time.

"It's okay, Mix," Della finally murmured as the hate began to recede, soothed by the repetitive folding and re-creasing of the paper tokens. The curse took in her emotion, tucked it hidden into the folds. Taking an action mattered, it soothed, even if the end result took years to arrive, being able to act made just a small bit of difference.

"It's not, please. That's us you're giving away, Lena and I. Don't do it."

"Mix. Do you think Lena would agree with that sentiment?" Della genuinely didn't know if the long-necked Gira would have agreed or not, but she needed Mix to stop and think. To use her mind for the moment so that Della could finish her task.

Della kept up the rhythm of folds. The pattern she'd created had been complicated, just as Lena and Mix had been complicated. As she worked she drifted from her original design, changing the angle of one fold here, one fold there. The differences were subtle. Della expanded the story of the two young lovers, layered in the betrayal of family, taking advantage of their tragedy. Della made her case in line and crease for anyone who could read the pattern. She didn't know if Mix saw the changes, if she could see the curse that Della layered into the Fancy design. True to his word, Papap had shown her how to add the secret folds. Anyone who tried to fold this pattern would be left only with the cursed version instead.

"There." Della made the last fold and with the smallest of her fingers, popped the pattern into place. She pushed the finished Fancy across the table to the Riuu.

The Riuu consulted with the voice in its ear and came back with a complaint.

"It don't look the same. Not exactly."

"The original pattern was designed as a standalone." Della explained. "It's a Posey, not a Fancy. Something to wear in your hair or adorn your coat. I've made structural changes to it so that it can be incorporated into a Fancy. That's what your employers want, right, something exclusive?"

The Riuu conferred quietly with the tinny squeak in its ear, then turned to pluck the drone from the air like an angry horsefly. Della had never met one, but in her long, strange lexicon of curses they figured prominently alongside fleas and bedbugs.

Della took that as assent.

"It will do. Our business is concluded." He handed the contract to Della, the long, glacile script of the Riuu declaring Lena's debt paid in full. The tiny lines and microdots made her eyes water, but Della could read it if she squinched her eyes just right.

"Done and done." Della nodded at the smaller Riuu who had retreated well out of Mix's reach. "Give Mix her posey back."

It obeyed, sidling towards the angry sibling, box held out in the very tips of its pincers, holding the rest of its armored body well out of the way. Mix took the box with ill grace and stomped a foot at the Riuu, who scuttled aside. She returned to the chair, cradling the box, casting poisonous looks at Della.

"A pleasure doing business with you." The larger Riuu pushed a token across the table. "If you need a negotiator in the future, I offer a discount to any and all parties I have dealt with in the past."

Della took the token, struck by the absurdity of it, of business and extortion and family and the small hope that Mix might eventually be able to understand.

"Do you know what you've done?" Della's younger sib began to rail as soon as the Riuu had left the room. "That was her *family* that paid him. Lena's family. They couldn't pass it up. They took it when they closed out h/her line, they took everything, incinerated everything that made up Lena except this one thing."

"So that's where you've been? Trying to steal that pattern back?" Della approached and took a moment to appraise the long thin rope that had been used to tether Mix to the chair. Riuu knots were simple, but human fingers could pick them apart easily enough. She settled down on her knees to begin.

"You made it for us. Me and Lena. Just us. And now you've given it, you've given US away. Don't you see that?" Mix was in tears.

"I don't think they're going to get any real satisfaction from that version of the fold." Della said quietly in the face of her sister's meltdown.

"That version." Mix glared at Della, red-rimmed eyes looking for the answer. "What do you mean 'that version' Della? What did you do?"

SIX

"Excuse me."

Della looked up from the stack of folded tokens she was sorting. The Gira that sidled up to the counter in the family shop was tall, almost tall enough to brush the ceiling with the branched tips of h/his ears. H/his warm yellow skin, mottled with deeper oranges and browns from the 5th season sun meant h/he was older, matriculation long past. H/He was a friend of Papap's, one of the few that bought Fancy for the stories, not the symmetry. H/He collected them like books, hung them on the walls of his home.

"Of course, can I help you?" Della swept the sorted tokens off the counter and into their bucket. Mix had finally matriculated and Della had begun training Wink, one of the younger cousins, to handle the knot-work. Della had taken to folding extra tokens in the between times so they would be ready to thread when Wink got out of school for the day.

"I hope so. Your grandfather created a beautiful Fancy for our child's matriculation a few years ago. We'd like him to do the same for our second child." H/He placed a pressed paper box on the counter and popped the lid open. "Something along these lines."

The timing could not have been worse. Mix emerged from the back of the shop, arms full of Fancy, just in time to see the poisoned fold topple out onto the countertop. Della's heart dropped at the fleeting expressions that chased across her younger sibling's face. Her own anger, the hate flashed back to the fore, a momentary pain before it settled back into the dull ache that had underscored every expression since the rescue two years before.

The "gifted" fancy fold first popped up in Lena's she/brother's shop at the next matriculation and, as Della had envisioned, the curse revealed itself to anyone who could read. It was stunning, a spiky emboldened mass of blues and greens among the sleeker forms of the usual Gira token folds. It caused a stir, a rush on that particular shop. It was hailed as the first in a new style and for a time, it could be found in only one place. The family had flourished. Where Lena had been declared a dead-line, Bishok, Lena's she/brother had redeemed the family fortunes.

Della knew it would only be a matter of time before someone went looking to get a copy made, she just hadn't expected that seeing it would make her feel quite so betrayed.

"Let me give you some advice, old friend." Papap came out from the back of the shop and turned the fold over in his fingertips carefully before returning it to the box. "This is not a Fancy you wish to give to your children."

"It says something awful, doesn't it? I've heard the rumors."

"It is...." Papap paused, the creases around his eyes shifted, telling their own story of warring emotion. "It is unlucky at best, cursed at worst. It is a stolen Imported pattern."

"That explains why none of the other Imported shops would touch it." The Gira closed the lid carefully, long thin fingers resting on the box. "You've heard the rumors, I presume?"

Della mirrored Papap's expression of surprise without really feeling it. Mix bustled past, moving to hang the armful of completed Fancy on the walls of the shop. Her gaze lingered on the box when she thought Della wasn't looking, short sharp glances over her shoulder.

"Rumors?" Della asked.

"The curse." H/He closed the box, sealing the Fancy away. Della felt the fire in her chest loosen, ebb a little. "Every student who received this Fold in a Fancy has failed to raise after matriculation. First it was only a few, last year ten, this year it is being gifted to twenty more."

Papap snorted. "There were over two hundred matriculations last year, there are always those who fail to rise."

The Gira shrugged. "You know as well as I that rumor requires no truth, only coincidence."

Della felt vaguely ill, then steeled her resolve. The curse she had folded, the hate she had imbued the pattern with, that had been for Mix, for Lena. It had been directed at Lena's family, not to the Gira. Not to the other students, innocent bystanders. She wasn't sure what she had expected. Somewhere in the back of her mind the idea that the Fancy itself would somehow rise up and punish Bishok for the insult had hung like a teenage revenge fantasy. In the intervening year Mix had watched, miserable, as Lena's family had flourished and Della's revenge had begun to emerge in collateral damage, all the while leaving Lena's family seemingly untouched.

A curse requires intent, it requires follow up to bring it to pass. Papap's words came back, a reminder. *It is a declaration of intent, not magic into and of itself.*

"Why so many?" Papap asked. "Surely the value is in the scarcity of the pattern? It's exclusivity?" He gave Della a stern look. They had argued back and forth about the pattern more than once already, Mix had sided with the old man, insisting she withdraw the curse, insisting there was something she could do to make it right. Della had resisted.

"The family fortunes are falling, simple as that. You wouldn't know it to look at the Family, of course. Fashions change and this was the only new pattern Bishok ever came up with. Add that to the rumor and…" The Gira gave an elaborate shrug. H/He tucked the box with the cursed fancy away. Della watched it go, quashed the urge to snatch it back and toss it into the fireplace.

"So, my friend, enough depressing things for today. Let me tell you about my she/daughter, see if you can come up with something unique and well, safer, for her matriculation next year."

SEVEN

"I'm not sure I understand. Are you refusing to negotiate?"

The Riuu sat across from Della and Mix, pincer arm resting comfortably under the table, smaller manipulating digits fiddling with the remains of the tea cakes. Two years was hardly enough time to see a change in a species that lived as long as the Riuu. A chip here and there, a lightening on the horny ridges of its carapace, but otherwise it looked exactly the same as their last meeting.

"What is there to negotiate for? It's hardly my fault that they failed to learn the Fancy pattern properly." Della sipped her own tea, disappointed that the small cups cooled so quickly, even in the 5th Season heat. "I traded in good faith, even though you were holding my little sister hostage. I even went one step further and gave them a proper Fancy instead of the Posey. I went above and beyond the terms, and now they want something more?"

"But the Fancy you gave them could not be copied."

Mix raised her eyebrows. "Then what have they been selling for the past three years? Again. Not our problem. You recorded the whole thing with your drone. They signed off of the exchange. There's nothing more to say."

"Our client is willing to be generous…"

"Generous? Which of our family are you going to hold hostage next? What new piece of our history do they want to extort?" In the intervening years, Della's contempt had crystallized. The strange, sharp pattern of the cursed Fancy had been all the rage for five full turns of the seasons, its presence reminding Mix every year of the circumstances of her loss until the younger sib had simply stayed off-planet for three months of the year. It was about the same time that the story Della told in angry folded paper had finally struck home, to Della's immense satisfaction. The Imported families quietly removed their support of Bishok. The thread-spinners and the box-makers, the kids who normally served apprenticeships to gain an insight into Gira Fancy-folding, all the substructure that went along with the business of Fancy-making stepped aside and Bishok's business went from thriving to expensive niche then slid into retro curiosity. The students who received the Fancy, from the best and brightest of the Gira families, failed to rise after matriculation. Della had hardened her heart as one by one the cursed children began to die, sometimes by their own hand, sometimes through strange circumstance. Mix though, Mix had a harder time with the collateral deaths. She quietly sent funerary tokens to the families, even the ones who'd turned their backs on Lena. Della knew and made a point of collecting news of every misfortune, every death in an attempt to cheer her younger sister, to show her that Bishok was well and truly being punished with the long, slow death of his livelihood.

This year the cursed Fancy failed to appear in any of the shops, Bishok's or otherwise, and a small corner of Della's soul was relieved. Maybe Mix would finally be able to stand up to try again without the constant reminders.

"They are looking for a new, unique pattern for the matriculation of Bishok's first child. It is not unheard of for Imported families to create new folds on request. Think of this as a commission."

"Let me ask you this." Della set the teacup down soundlessly. "Why me?"

"You were requested."

"Yes. But why? There are three other Imported Fancy-makers in town, any of those families should be happy to take a generous commission."

The Riuu clattered his pincer under the table. "The other families turned the offer down."

"Seems strange, doesn't it. Every other family turning down such a lucrative offer? And now Bishok only has me left to deal with. More tea?" Della lifted the clay pot and held it just off the table until the negotiator acquiesced.

"Yes, please. You have assessed the situation perfectly, but my job here is to broker understanding. I am here to find out what you want."

"Want. What does Bishok have that we could possibly want?" Mix interjected.

"Despite their recent troubles, s/his Family is not without influence. And while Dispossessed Lena's death was tragic, they were not directly responsible."

"No." Mix's tone was sharp and flat. The sound brought the Riuu up short.

"I beg your pardon?"

"Not Dispossessed Lena. Just. Lena. I *get* that this is how the Gira refer to the children who fail to rise, I get it better than most, but to bully her memory, to keep after her after she's dead that is JUST TOO MUCH. That needs to stop. ALL OF THIS needs to stop." Mix had risen. Her hands gripped the tabletop like she was preparing to flip it over in her frustration. Della put out a hand to steady her sib, only to have it pushed aside.

The Riuu angled its eyestalks in her direction and clacked its pincers thoughtfully. "My dear, part of my job is to understand the wants and needs of both sides of a negotiation. What Bishok wants, really wants, is not a bit of Fancy folded paper. It is a way to make a connection with you, to open communication with his older sibling's one true love. What you need… Well, perhaps I have an idea about that as well."

EIGHT

"Ninety percent of the Gira won't be able to read it, you know. Adding another fold to the mix won't simply make everything stop." Della added the second token, lining up the holes so the light passed through them and painted dots on the rug under her feet.

"I know. But it's not really for them, not for all of them anyway. It's for me. And Lena. And even Bishok. And…I think it's for you too." Mix stirred her fingers around in the bucket of crisp-edged tokens, looking for just the right color. "I have to stand up to try again. I can't keep marking time like this."

"Do you really think Bishok is deserving of your forgiveness?" Della stomped hard on her own emotions, trying to keep the acid out of her tone. Mix knew where Della's opinion lay. Were it up to Della, she would have simply refused every overture and let the curse grind to its bitter conclusion.

Della set the second fold, then the third. She and Mix had gone over every idea, every moment of Lena and Mix's lives that had stayed bright through the intervening years. Della had tried to find forgiveness in her own heart, tried to let the love for her sister flow into the new token fold she was creating.

Mix sighed and finally fished a blue token from the barrel, turning it over in her fingers. "I don't really give a shit," she said finally. "Five years I've wasted on hating Lena's younger sib. Five years I have been miserable, counting every death, every turn of misfortune, waiting for it all to add up to be enough. Do you know what I finally figured out Della?"

Della twisted and popped the fold, expanding the paper petals like those on a ripening flower. They resisted, cutting back and rearing into sharp spikes. Della dropped the Fancy, startled. Mix picked it up with two fingers and casually tossed it into the fireplace, then handed the blue token to Della to start again.

"I figured out that there is no magic number. No finite amount of tragedy that will ever make what happened to Lena right. I'm the one that has to set the end point. I have to be the one who decides when to let it go."

Della frowned and began the folds again, left over right, carefully creasing, burnishing the fold with the back of a fingernail to make sure it set. "Do you think Lena would be able to forgive?" She added in a second token, this one a pale yellow with bright red ink. Della took a deep breath and twisted, pressing with fingertips and knuckles. The Fancy popped again, erupting into spikes and jagged edges that nicked her fingertips and drew blood.

"I get to decide when it's over Della. Not you." Mix handed her a fresh token and tossed the latest attempt into the fire. "Please try again."

Della took the token she was handed, this time a brighter green, foxed with lily white, and made a new fold, carefully selecting the leading edge and turning it under.

"Forgiveness isn't really my thing." Della pointed out. "He stole your lives, Mix, he stole the one thing left of you and Lena and then he had you held hostage until I gave s/him what s/he wanted."

The folded token curled under her fingers, the clean-cut edge nicking the inside of her thumb. This time Della flicked it into the fire before Mix could touch it.

"S/He stole a piece of paper, Della. It was a very special piece of paper, but it wasn't the sum of our time together. I was young, and I was in mourning and I should have let it go, rather than letting our revenge poison all my happy memories of Lena."

Della selected a new token herself, a darker color, a darker place to begin. "Mix, you know creating a new Fancy isn't going to magically fix everything. You can't present this to Bishok and *poof* everything will go back to the way it was."

Mix selected the second token, not much brighter than the first, and passed it over. "I don't expect magic, Della, but I am hoping to find a little peace. Bishok said something nice. He's waiting to see what we say back."

Della took a long breath in, fingers holding the folded tokens into place. A long breath out took away some of the burning in the pit of her stomach. She closed her eyes, imagining the look on Mix's face when Lena had walked out of the matriculation ceremony, wreathed in Fancy, ready to start their new lives together. She held onto that image until the hateful burning faded just a bit more. Then another fold, then another image. Della worked her way through the paper folds, adding brighter tokens as she went.

❀

ABOUT THE AUTHOR

Kimberly created her first videogame back when the 80-column card was the new hot thing. This turned a literary love of science fiction into a full blown obsession with the intersection of technology and humanity. Kimberly currently works in mobileVR/AR game development studio, lectures on the intersection of art and code for UCSC's master's degree program in Games and Playable Media and writes science fiction about how all these app-driven superpowers are going to change the human race. You can find her on Twitter at @Ing3nu or on her blog at **www.ungerink.com**.